Churchill's Secret Saboteurs

Les McLaughlan

Published by Les McLaughlan, 2023.

This is a work of fiction. Similarities to real people, places, or events are entirely coincidental.

CHURCHILL'S SECRET SABOTEURS

First edition. August 4, 2023.

Copyright © 2023 Les McLaughlan.

ISBN: 979-8223692867

Written by Les McLaughlan.

Also by Les McLaughlan

Project Damocles
Spandau Citadel
Craigmarr's Lament
Churchill's Secret Saboteurs

A special thanks to my wife Linda for editing my manuscript.

Chapter 1

The outside door to the small Norwegian Alpine hut swung open, and the snow and wind howled in. Major Andrew Hughes had to put all his weight behind the door to force it shut. Brushing the snow off his combat jacket, he strode to the small group standing by the wood-burning fire.

"Ian, you can't be serious about this proposal."

"I'm deadly serious, Sir," replied the young Lieutenant.

"Deadly is the right word. Putting aside your slim chance of surviving for the moment, what about the Norwegian Government's directive. The one ordering us, and I repeat, not to ambush or assassinate any German officers. The Norwegian government fear, and with justification, heavy reprisals. The Germans have already taken brutal reprisals against other local communities. So, tell me how you think we can get away with this ambush?"

"That road is notorious. In the last ten years before the war, more than a dozen tourists have died in road accidents on that twisted stretch, particularly at this time of year. My plan is simply to add to those statistics, Major. Let me run through my proposal before you dismiss it."

Lieutenant Ian Anderson laid the map of the mountain road on the table. Methodically he traced out the route the German convoy would take and the regular time frame they used. The others watching followed Ian's finger as he skimmed the road and stopped at a double S-bend. He went on to outline the German vehicle protocol used to minimise any chance of an ambush succeeding. Vehicles in hostile areas must maintain a one-hundred-meter distance. With that spacing the Commandant's car would be the only vehicle on either side of the double S-bend. That is where I've planned for the accident to happen. The locals cannot be held responsible for the Commandant's vehicle smashing through the safety barrier and skidding off the road."

"I am not sure they always keep that distance apart," the Major said.

"They definitely do on this stretch of the road because they know if the personnel carrier skidded into the staff car, it would either crush it against the cliff or push it over the barrier."

"Okay, but how do you ensure they go into a skid at the right point. And before you answer that, how can you be sure the barrier doesn't stop them from going over, what I agree, is a sheer drop?"

Ian looked straight at the Major, an officer he had only recently met, and had quickly grown to admired.

"I, or rather we, will have compacted the snow on the road. The surface will be swept, leaving a clear ice surface. As to the barriers, the existing bolts will be replaced with damaged, rusted ones. When the vehicle has a tyre blowout, at the critical time, the car will be sent into a spin, smashing through the barrier."

"Let me work through this. The road surface would be compacted the night before, leaving a thick layer of ice invisible to the eye. And the barrier pre-weakened, but how do you guarantee the blowout at that exact point? Because there are no places where a sniper could take that shot from with any accuracy."

"Here," Ian pointed to the map again. "There's a ledge with an overhang. From there, I can see the bend clearly and take the shot that will blow out the front tyre, sending the car into an uncontrollable spin in only one possible direction, the barrier."

Major Hughes said nothing, well, not at first. He had grown to like this young Lieutenant who displayed excellent strategy skills. Hughes, a professional soldier, though not one of the usual officer class. He had been attached to this off-shoot of Military Intelligence working on unconventional warfare research MI(R). That was where he met their current commanding officer, Colonel Colin Gubbins. Gubbins had been given command of four independent companies with the task of forming an irregular force to harass and resist the Nazi occupation of Norway. But recently, the chiefs of staff in Whitehall had ordered them to strictly adhere to the Norwegian G\governments directives. He had likened that to fighting with one hand tied behind your back.

"First of all," Hughes asked, "how do you know the ledge will hold you? And how can you be sure you could hit your target from there?"

"I have checked out the ledge. It is solid, with an overhang that gives me cover from above and an excellent anchor point. I can take the shot from this vantage point on the ledge."

"And then what?"

"I hide under the overhang until it's safe to come out."

"If they keep their troops there for any length of time, you will most likely freeze to death."

"Sir, I am relying on them assessing the incident and then returning to their camp. I can't believe they will keep people freezing on the mountain for no practical purpose."

"What if they do? You will not be able to show yourself, and you will freeze to death."

"That's a risk I am prepared to take."

Chapter 2

It was starting to get light when they replaced the last of the barrier bolts and finalised compacting the snow. As the morning light started to break through, the team prepared to withdraw.

"Remember Sir, you have to blow out the front tyre just as the vehicle reaches that slight slope, past the fourth post," the Company Sergeant reminded Ian for the third time.

"Thank you, George. I will remember."

Ian took one last look at the bend, checked his anchor points, then slid down to his position on the ledge at the side of the mountain. He pressed himself into a corner on the ledge, again checking his anchor point. He knew his sleeping bag would only give him some protection from the chilling winds. Ian knew he had to conserve his energy, and critically preserve his body heat. For once, he was grateful to rely on the disciplined German transport schedules. If everything goes to plan, the convoy will arrive within the hour.

Ian hoped his Norwegian army comrades had managed to disable the lead German scout car. He'd studied the German's convoy routine and knew their travel formation dictated that a scout car would take the lead, followed by the Commandant's vehicle, with the personnel carrier taking up the rear-guard position. Ian knew his time to take the shot would be much tighter if the scout car still travelled in front. But he knew, he would still take the shot regardless. Still, if they had successfully managed to incapacitate the vehicle, and he really hoped they had, he would have a longer window of time to take his shot. He knew, for safety reasons, the personnel carrier would not enter the bend until they could see the staff car had cleared it, and, was waiting for them further down the road.

Down in the town centre, the convoy was getting ready to travel to the next occupied sector. The troops were on board the personnel carrier as the Commanding officer stepped from the hotel he was using as his quarters. Looking around, he saw the troops in their vehicle, but the scout car driver had his head stuck under the bonnet of his car and seemed to be pulling at cables.

"What's the hold-up?" demanded the officer.

"The car will not start, but everything looks okay."

"Get it started," he barked at the car's driver.

"Do you want me to get the others down until we are ready to go?" asked the personnel carrier's driver.

"No. Keep them where they are."

"Sir."

Ten minutes later, with all the troops shivering in the personnel carrier, the Commandant decided to leave without the scout car. He ordered a motorbike with a sidecar to drive in the lead position. They were sure the road would be deserted. Still, for added security, the scout car's machine gun and gunner travelled in the passenger seat next to the staff car's driver. The Commandant's second-in-command would have to travel in the personnel carrier, having given up his seat for the machine gunner now positioned in the front of the staff car.

"Have them join us when that idiot fixes his vehicle," ordered the Commandant.

"Yes, Sir," said the intimidated officer as the staff car drove off.

From behind the shed, next to the general store, the Norwegian who had disabled the scout car flashed a mirrored signal that the convoy was en route.

Ian re-positioned himself close to the rear of the ledge under the overhang, which gave him a degree of shelter from the northerly winds. He knew he would hear the convoy in plenty of time for him to creep out to his already chosen firing position. If, and he hoped not, the scout car was still running, he would be in that exposed position for longer. But if the first car is the staff car, he will only have been exposed for a few minutes.

Ian thought he was used to cold weather when as a teenager, he had a job delivering milk in the early hours of winter mornings in Glasgow. Still, nothing prepared him for the freezing Norwegian mountains. The locals said he would get used to it, but he knew better. His mind wandered, and he thought of his family back home. Ian's elder brother Frank was somewhere in Belgium with the British Expeditionary Force, and he knew his mother would be worried sick for the both of them. His father had been too young to enlist at the start of the first world war. By 1916 he was working in the shipyards building Navy ships, and although he wanted to, he was not allowed to join up when he turned 18. Ian's father always felt guilty for not doing his bit when he saw friends who had served. Some resented that he did not serve, but others, real friends, never held it against him. Still, he could not shake the guilt he felt and wanted to make a point of taking both his sons, in their uniforms, to his local pub for a pint. When they returned from the pub that night, his mother served them their dinner and then went straight to bed. Ian could see she had been crying, but what struck him most was the cold stare she gave his smiling father.

The sound of a motorbike, followed by grinding gears from struggling vehicles, pulled him back to the present. After quickly checking his silenced pistol, he carefully crept forward into his chosen firing position. Ian knew he would have to take his gloves off to grip the pistol properly for an accurate shot. He was not prepared for how cold the gun felt in his hands. And remembered the reports of weapons being stuck to their owner's bare skin as though someone had glued or welded them together.

The motorbike cleared the second bend as the staff car rounded the first, and now approached the second. But the driver was travelling much slower than expected. Now Ian worried that the weakened barrier might still stop them from going over the edge. As the car approached the critical section, the vehicle started sliding sideways, and the driver panicked and overcorrected. The vehicle started to pick up speed as Ian fired two bullets into the front left tyre. The impact was immediate, the car slew to the side then started spinning out of control and smashed into the weakened barrier and slipped off the edge of the road. Ian started to slide back to his ledge when he saw the vehicle stop with the rear over the edge. The front sticking up in the air, prevented from going over by one of the barriers fence posts jammed against the gearbox.

Ian was stunned. *The personnel carrier will be able to winch that back, and they are bound to see the bullet holes. It won't take them long to find out where the shot was taken from. At best, I will be a prisoner of war, but that's not very likely.*

The driver of the personnel carrier had worried about the length of time it was taking the staff car to clear the bend. He decided to drive slowly around and immediately took in the scene before him. The officer beside him ordered the driver to stop. They both jumped out of the cab. Right away, the driver started to prepare the winch as the officer approached the staff car. Looking through the window, he could see the fear written on all their faces. He held up both hands and told them to sit still. In the back seat, one of the officers must have moved, and the car rocked slowly back and then righted itself again.

"Stop, don't move, or you will all go over the edge," screamed the officer.

The driver and others from the personnel carrier were running out the winch cable when again, the vehicle screeched and rocked backwards before settling. Then they heard it, quiet at first, but the unmistakable screech of metal against metal as the car inched back.

Suddenly the driver's door swung open, and he threw himself onto the verge.

"No," screamed the officer, but in that instance the occupants inside the car all knew their inevitable fate. The vehicle rocked violently up and down before tipping backwards and plummeting down the mountainside. For a moment, everyone stood silently, then the young officer unhooked his holster and drew out his Luger.

"Please no. Please no." pleaded the driver

The officer fired three times before re-holstering his pistol.

"Get rid of him."

No one moved; they just stared at the body.

"That coward cost all of them their lives. And I refuse to take his body back for burial." Again no one stepped forward. The officer started to unhook his holster again, then stopped. Slowly he walked over to the body, grabbed a leg and started to drag it towards the edge. The platoon Sergeant stepped forward and grabbed the other leg. When they reached the edge, they slipped the body over.

"Thank you, sergeant."

"Sir."

"Get the men to rig up a temporary barrier until we can get it repaired."

"Can we light a fire to keep everyone from freezing to death while we make this repair?"

"Of course."

In the confusion Ian had managed to crawl back to his hiding point below the ledge's overhang. He was now starting to shiver and knew he would need to get out of there before he froze to death. While above him, the driver was very carefully backing up his carrier while others in a roster were either working to repair the barrier or standing around a 45-gallon drum with a roaring fire. Ian could hear the sound of wood burning, that crack that hot embers make. He knew he had to stay awake and hoped these troops would be gone soon and his men arrive.

Ian started to shake uncontrollably, worried he might be making a noise and could give his position away. His only hope was the noise from the fire, and the barrier repair work would drown out any noise he might be making.

He didn't notice the cold anymore. He had stopped shivering; in fact, he felt warm.

Are you ready for your dinner son?

Mum, is that you?

When did I get home?

"Ian, Ian, wake up, Ian."

"What, what's happening?"

"I've secured a rope around you, but I have to slip you over the ledge for the lads to be able to pull you up. Ian, do you understand?"

"Over the edge, for the lads to..."

"For the lads to pull you up."

He simply nodded.

Once they got Ian on the road, and into car they started to wrap him in warmer clothes.

"We need to get him off this mountain before he dies," said the company's medic. "And it's too far to the base. We will have to take him into the town."

"We can't risk that. Ian will stand a better chance at our base, but I will send word that we need a doctor urgently," replied Major Hughes.

Back at their base and after arranging for the doctor Hughes entered his makeshift office, he was met by his radio operator.

"Have you heard the news Sir??"

"What news?"

"They have started sending ships for us. We are being evacuated from tomorrow."

If only I had been given that news yesterday, I would never have approved Ian's proposal.

He, like everyone else, had heard the rumours, they ranged from major reinforcements arriving right through to the Germans making a tactical withdrawal to fight in France. Andrew Hughes hadn't thought they would abandon Norway to the Nazis.

"Who sent the message?"

"Brigadier Gubbins."

"Brigadier, did you say Brigadier? Gubbins"

"Yes Sir, apparently he's been recently promoted, and he wants you to contact him as soon as you arrive back home."

"Try and get him for me now."

"Sir."

"Major, I've got the Brigadier for you."

"Andrew, you got my message?" asked Gubbins.

"I did, but I don't understand why we are doing this right now. We, along with the French and Poles, have been able to engage and push the Jerries back, and with the right support, we can push them even further. We've regained control of Narvik. It's an ice-free harbour, and the navy can sail right in and resupply us and...."

"Andrew, things are worse than you may know. They have ended the evacuation at Dunkirk. It was a heroic achievement. Unfortunately, we have had to leave many of our people behind and most of the French army. Our equipment is scattered all over French beaches. The Germans know we are in a very weakened state, and Hitler will pounce. That is why we are pulling you out now."

"Surely, if we stayed here, we could force the Jerries to expend troops fighting us."

"Andrew the Jerries are racing through France as we speak and can't hold out much longer. That's why we are calling all our companies back for re-deployment preparing for a blitzkrieg invasion."

Andrew Hughes remembered their earlier, rushed orders. A hastily thrown-together expeditionary force of ten Independent Companies. Territorial units, not the regular army, were sent to Norway to fight a guerrilla-style warfare under the command of the then Colonel Gubbins.

"Andrew, I have requested you and young Anderson to be posted to work with me."

"What about our Company?"

"I have seen the report and have made some recommendations, which Churchill himself supports. Basically, the ten Independent Companies will be wound up, and many of the troops will be redeployed. The others will have the option of joining a new special unconventional force, a Commando unit.

"I assume I will be playing a part of that force."

"That's what we need to discuss when you return to London."

Before leaving his makeshift office to see Ian, Andrew briefed his fellow officers and senior NCOs. He was in deep contemplation as he made his way to the medical hut, leaving the others to prepare everyone for disembarking.

"Doctor, is the Lieutenant fit to travel?"

"Definitely not."

"How serious are his injuries. Is he suffering from frostbite?"

"It's a bit early to say, but he certainly, has ice burns, and he has lost skin on his cheek where he must have been stuck to ice on the mountain. That wound and the ice burns could become infected."

"Doctor, you know things are very fluid, and regrettably, I have to evacuate my position here?"

"Evacuate. A nice word, but don't you mean abandon your position?"

Andrew shrugged.

"Major, I have heard the rumours. Is it true the King and the Government have already left for England?"

"I am not sure, but if they haven't, they will leave soon."

"And the French have already gone. It is only you and the Poles who are left?"

"Not for long."

"I understand. Will your government evacuate Narvik because if they don't, the Germans will make an example of the whole population here?"

"I know my commanding officer has taken up the matter, and he fights very hard. But I can't lie. I have just received orders to evacuate my men starting tomorrow. So, back to my question, will he be fit to travel even with severe frostbite?"

"I am not overly worried about the frostbite, and if that was my only concern, I would have no problem. My main concern is severe hypothermia. His core temperature dropped to around 90 degrees fahrenheit, about 32 degrees centigrade. He is having trouble breathing and has bouts of severe shivering. When I managed to speak with him, his speech was slurred, and he clearly is suffering from some degree of memory loss. If that boy had been there any longer, you would have been bringing back a corpse. So, to answer your question, he cannot be moved until he stabilises."

"We are only talking days, Doctor."

"He is young and strong. Speak to me tomorrow."

Chapter 3

When Major Hughes arrived back at his hut he saw a group of officers standing around the wood-burning fire. They were not socialising; they were in deep discussion about the complex logistics of the company's evacuation.

"Gentlemen, we have to be out of here by the 8th of June."

"That only gives us four days to pack up everything."

"What about the others. The French, Poles, and Norwegian army?"

"The French have already started evacuating and will take some of the Poles with them. We will take the remainder and any Norwegian troops that want to come."

"Will the Norwegian troops be allowed to evacuate?"

"There is no point in them staying and becoming prisoners of war. They should evacuate and form an exiled Norwegian army," replied Hughes.

"What about the civilians, Sir?" asked one of the young officers. "I mean, they really supported us."

"I can't confirm, and it's not supported by Whitehall, but I understand discussions are taking place with the fishing fleet owners to evacuate all those who want to leave."

"Sir, we could hold...."

Hughes cut across the young lieutenant. "It's not a matter of whether we could, or could not, hold Narvik. The decision has been made, and we start our evacuation tomorrow."

Early the following day, Major Hughes made his way to the sick bay.

"So, doctor, will Ian be okay to move within the next few days?"

"He seems much better today. More coherent. And physically more stable. I would have liked a longer recovery, but given the circumstances, he will be fit enough to travel."

Andrew felt as though a weight had been lifted from his shoulders. Smiling at the doctor, he asked if it was okay to talk to him.

"Of course."

"And doctor, I would like you to travel with him on the ship."

"That is out of the question."

"Why?"

"Because I will be needed here to look after my patients."

"The Germans will..."

"They will want the port operating again. They will need local labour, all-be-it forced labour. But they will need these workers; they and their families have been my patients for years. So, I will not be joining you on your ship."

"I understand."

Back at his own headquarters Major Hughes called an officers' and NCOs' meeting. On the walls were a series of maps and drawings of all the critical infrastructure around Narvik.

"I want a plan by tonight on what needs to be destroyed to cripple the port's operations."

Hughes left his officers pouring over the drawings while he went and met with the port town Mayor.

The two men stood facing each other. Both understood the significance of the meeting. Major Hughes wanted to say sorry, but he knew that would make no difference. The last time they met was when the allies had repelled the German forces, and both men were elated. Now it was a different kind of reception.

"I am sure you are aware of what is happening," Hughes said.

"You are leaving us to the Germans."

"Yes." Andrew wanted to say much more but knew that would only be platitudes. Yes, was the only honest answer.

"What do you want from me?"

"I want to find out what we can do to minimise your town's suffering."

The Mayor took a few steps away from Hughes towards the door, then shaking his head, turned to face Andrew. "What are you planning to do before you leave?"

"Damage as much port facility as possible."

"You are going to blow up my town, but you want my absolution for your act."

"My orders are to destroy all infrastructure," he paused. "But I want to leave essential services, so I will need the help of your town engineers."

"Go on."

Andrew knew he should not be discussing his orders with the Mayor of a town that was eminent to fall under German control. He knew he should be overseeing the total destruction of the port town of Narvik. Andrew also knew he would be court-martialled if this conversation was ever repeated. *In for a penny, In for a pound*, he thought.

"I want to find a way to keep power to your hospital but render industrial power useless. I want to ensure your people have as many supplies as we can give them because we will destroy key rail and bridge infrastructure. I want to minimise the hurt on your people."

"Very admirable, but you're still deserting us."

"I don't have the time to debate the right and wrong of the situation. I just need your cooperation to minimise the impact of our evacuation on the town."

Again, the two men looked into each other's eyes. But this time, the Mayor saw a younger man in anguish, wanting to help. He felt ashamed of the way he had approached what was a genuine attempt to mitigate the damage this officer was about to inflict on the town.

"Please wait here, and I will fetch the town planner and chief engineer."

"Mayor, I am stepping out on a limb here. My orders are clear. I have to destroy all key infrastructure. If my superiors knew I was even discussing our evacuation, I would be relieved of my command."

"I understand the need for secrecy."

Ten minutes later, the three men returned to the Mayor's office with a bundle of files. They spent the next hour drawing up a list of jobs that needed to be carried out before the final troops left. The first two items that needed to be secured were an electrical supply to the hospital and the water treatment plant. The chief engineer insisted on involving the chief electrical superintendent. And, although Major Hughes was unhappy about bringing in another person, he accepted the logic of the proposal.

After informing the superintendent of the situation and pacifying his outrage at the news that his power station was about to be destroyed, they set about how to minimise critical upheaval. The most important concern was ensuring continuous electrical power to the town's hospital. This would require an extra emergency backup generator with a substantial diesel supply. Next was the water treatment plant, requiring similar arrangements. Luckily all homes had wood-burning fires for cooking and heating. The fire was also to heat water for the homes.

The group continued working through the items on their hastily produced agenda. Each house will be allocated a supply of lamp oil. Major Hughes said they would leave all their food supplies for the council to distribute. As the meeting ended, Major Hughes restated the importance of keeping these discussions private. The electrical superintendent stood up.

"I have a proposal, Major."

"What's your proposal?"

"Please hear me out. I know your orders are to blow up the power station. And I understand why and accept you will carry out your orders. However, you could destroy the current operating power plant rendering it incapable of generating electricity without destroying the old, decommissioned plant. I could rig up a temporary supply from the old plant to the hospital and water treatment plant. The output from the small plant would minimise the need to use the emergency generators unless the old power plant dies."

"That would still leave the Germans with electrical power."

"It is an ancient and small generator set, of little use to them, but saves the hospital relying solely on diesel generators."

Andrew knew agreeing to this proposal would go against his specific orders to destroy the power station. But his gut reaction was telling him to agree. *Emergency generators are for when the power fails. They are not meant to be the source of supply.*

"Set it up."

"Thank you, Major," said the grateful Mayor.

Back at his HQ, Major Hughes called an officers' and NCOs' meeting to obtain an update on the evacuation status. He was surprised to see Lieutenant Anderson sitting at a desk in the office. The maps on the wall had different pins in place, each depicting a structure to be destroyed. Each pin was allocated the number of squad members depending on the size of the task.

"All the teams have been briefed and will be activated tomorrow," reported Captain Smith.

"I want to meet with the team tasked with the power plant demolition in half an hour."

"I'll arrange that right now."

Andrew walked over to the desk Ian Anderson was sitting at. "What are you doing here, and why are you not still in the hospital?"

"The doctor is a lovely caring man who was genuinely worried about me, but I am in better shape than he thought. I know I was out of it for a while, but I am okay, honestly, Major."

"Then I want you to oversee the power plant demolition."

Andrew Hughes went on to outline the meeting he had earlier that evening. He then told Ian what he had agreed to and why. Ian sat mulling over what Major Hughes had said.

"That decision goes against our orders to destroy key infrastructure which could be of benefit to the Germans."

"I, and I know you, don't like the fact that we are evacuating Narvik. We both know with the right support, we could hold this and other northern regions. But reluctantly, we must obey orders and pull out. Ian, I don't want to leave the doctor relying on diesel generators if I don't have to. So, I am giving you a direct order to ensure the current operating plant generators are permanently put out of action but leaving the old, decommissioned plant untouched."

At the same time Andrew Hughes was briefing Lieutenant Anderson, the electrical supervisor was briefing his small, hand-picked crew of electricians and linesmen.

"I have brought you here to help me redirect supply from the old plant to the hospital and the water treatment plant."

One of the linesmen said that would have been easy in the past, but we took out all the old links and pathways when the new power station came online. The terminations and joints have been removed. He did not think it was feasible to reinstate. Well, not without a lot of rerouting of high-voltage lines.

"How long would it take to make the necessary changes? "Asked the superintendent.

"If we start tomorrow, about a week," said one of the linesmen.

"You have twenty-four hours."

"Impossible."

"Twenty-four hours, and when you finish, pack a case because you are leaving."

"Leaving for where?"

"Britain."

"Britain, for how long?"

"For the duration of the war."

"I am going nowhere. I have a wife and two daughters and...."

"Tell them to pack also."

"Why do we have to leave?"

"Because you are the only people with the local knowledge to re-establish the power system, leaving the Germans to start from scratch, with no drawings or understanding where the pits are."

"And you?" asked the other linesman.

"I will likewise have to leave, but only once we have completed our task.

The next few days flew in, and the evacuation was coming to an end. Before leaving, Major Hughes met with the Mayor and the hospital doctor.

"Are you sure I can't entice you to leave?" he asked.

"You can't, but thanks for the offer. Maybe we shall meet again," said the Mayor.

"I hope so. But until then, stay safe."

"You too Major Hughes.

Chapter 4

It had rained constantly from the moment the ship rounded the top of Scotland, sailing down the west coast. Still, even that could not wipe the smiles off the faces of the troops as they lined up to disembark when the ship tied up in Greenock. On the dock waiting for the ship's arrival were rows of three-ton army trucks. The troops would be taken to a holding station, and from there, they would be provided with either transport or travel documents. It was agreed that the men could have up to seventy-two hours to report back to the home barracks. For some, that gave them time to see their loved ones; for others, it was a drinking binge. With troops arriving back from Dunkirk only days before, the train system was overloaded.

"I don't think most of them will make it back to the barracks in seventy-two hours, do you, Sir?" asked Lieutenant Anderson.

"No, Ian, I think you're right. But what about you? Are you going home?"

"Glasgow is just up the road, so I will go home. Hopefully, my brother will be there."

"Your mother will be over the moon to see you both."

"I know, but it puts her on an emotional rollercoaster. Happy then sad."

"Ian, in this life, you have to grab the good times whenever you can. Enjoy your time with your family."

"What about you, Sir, time with your family?"

Andrew Hughes would have loved that, but Brigadier Gubbins had different plans. "If I am not mistaken, that staff car is waiting to take me to Central Station for the London train."

"Glasgow Central? Station?" asked Ian.

"Alright, get your kit bag," Andrew Hughes could not keep the smile off his face as Ian ran back to grab his kit.

When they arrived at the train station, the two men parted. Andrew for his meeting with the Brigadier and Ian to his parent's home in Maryhill.

Ian's mum stood at the sink peeling potatoes and talking to Frank. He had just arrived home after being evacuated from Dunkirk.

"Do you have to return to the barracks tonight?" she asked.

"No, they gave us 48-hour leave, and then I have to report back. But sure, it's only up the road anyway."

"Aye, that's handy," she smiled at her son.

There was a knock on the door. As Frank started to stand up, his dad said, sit down son. I'll get that. Seconds later, Frank's dad shouted. "Frank, it's someone for you."

"Don't go out tonight son. Stay here and have a drink with your dad and me."

As he left the small kitchen, he saw Ian with his finger to his lips. The two brothers had a quick hug as Ian passed. When he entered the kitchen, he saw his mum staring out the window.

"What are we having for dinner?"

"Sure, I told you, then she paused, Ian." She spun around as tears welled in her eyes. "Ian."

The two stood locked in each other's arms until dad spoke. "That's it, Peggy, get your coat on. We're going out with the boys for a drink. We'll eat later."

In London, the following day, Andrew met Brigadier Colin Gubbins outside Charing Cross Station.

"Let's walk along the river, Andrew."

"Sounds good to me, Brigadier?" Andrew smiled.

"I know, it was Churchill's idea to give the unit status. But between us, it's still Colin."

As they walked Andrew filled the Brigadier in on what had happened between his leaving Norway and Andrew's evacuation.

"I know it was difficult for you to leave, but orders are orders."

"But that's not why I'm here. Is it, Sir?"

"No, it's not. Let me buy you a drink."

It was just before lunchtime when the two men entered the bar. It was already crowded with groups of young men in various uniforms, Army, Navy, and a few Air Force pilots. Colin knew the bar would get louder as more and more troops arrived. Andrew managed to secure a table in the far corner.

"It's going to get noisy here," Andrew said.

"That will be fine."

Both men sat with their pint of Ale and a whisky. Colin placed his glass on the table. "France is beaten, and everyone in Whitehall expects Hitler to launch his invasion in the autumn or early next year. It's my view that Hitler would want to invade us as soon as possible, banking on us being demoralised after Dunkirk and Norway. However, there appear to be three options. The first, which Hitler leans towards, is to strike while the iron is hot and invade sometime in July. The second, Goring's position, is to let the Luftwaffe destroy the RAF before the invasion. I tend to agree with that one. And, a third view suggests some form of overture for peace. According to leaked information, Rudolf Hess has proposed that Germany enter into a peace pact with Britain. Then, we simply step back and let them concentrate all their forces against Russia, smashing communism in its infancy."

"What about their pact with Stalin."

"The Nazis hate Stalin and only tolerate him while it suits them."

"What does Churchill think?"

"That's what I want to discuss with you. Let me get you another drink, and I will tell you what Churchill wants."

"It's my round," Andrew said.

"Not today."

When the Brigadier returned with the drinks, he removed his jacket, clearly indicating this would take a while. He gave Andrew an overview of the defence preparedness, or more like the lack of preparedness. Telling him the civilian war effort is flat out, 24/7 producing planes for the RAF, ships for the navy and all manners of equipment for the army. The army is also frantically training thousands of recruits to fill the gaps left by those who never managed to get out from Dunkirk. But Churchill also wants us to establish a range of unconventional units under the Minister of Economic Warfare, Hugh Dalton. Brigadier Gubbins went on to tell Andrew the Minister was aware of his past services. Russia from 1919 to 1920 and Ireland from 1920 to 1922. Then the years he served with MI(R).

"I am not sure where you are going with this, Colin?"

"My orders are to put together a number of highly secret, special units using my past intelligence experience. A lot of which I picked up from the tactics of Michael Collins, the late Irish Republican Army leader."

"I can see that, but I want to stay with my company and fight the conventional way I've been taught."

"As I have already told you, your company, along with the other nine, are being disbanded and redeployed to other regiments."

"Not all of them?"

"Well, not quite. The War Office is disbanding the Independent Companies. But they will be establishing a new Commando Company."

"Then I want to be with the Commando Unit."

"The Commandos will need to be given special training, as will the new Auxiliary Units I am putting together."

"What role will these Auxiliary Units play, and what training will they need?"

"Our new Auxiliaries will go into hiding if or when an invasion happens. They will not carry out Home Guard duties but act as resistance cells. Frankly, it's estimated they will be lucky if they survive weeks. For public morale, we have to keep their very existence secret.

Only those who need to Know will be aware of their existence. And that is why I want you and young Ian to oversee that training."

"How long would you need me for?"

"I am not sure, but I really need you both."

"If I agree, will you agree to authorise our transfers when we want to leave?"

"Yes."

"When do you want us to start?"

"Both of you should take 72 hours' leave and then report for duty."

"What Barracks will we be working out of?"

"Initially, you will be working out of my planning office."

"In Whitehall?"

"No, I am set up in Baker Street."

"What 221B Baker Street?"

"No, I'm not Sherlock Holmes. We are set up at 64 Baker Street."

Chapter 5

After spending two days together as a family, Frank needed to report that morning to the Maryhill Barracks, where the current positions to deployment would be passed on. Although it was very early and raining, Ian decided to walk with him to the Barracks.

"Do you know where you have to report yet?" Frank asked.

"I am expecting a telegram with orders sometime today."

"Ian, I couldn't say anything at home, not to mum or dad, but I can't sleep. My mind continually reruns the scene on the beach. So many of our men, not men, boys, were chopped up by Stuka bombers as they stood chest high in the water. The water was dark red with floating bodies, but there was nowhere to run. If it wasn't for the RAF boys and those poor bastards left on the beach, I don't think anyone would have made it onto the boats."

Ian clearly saw the pain on his brother's face, and before he could say anything, Frank spoke again.

"So much for your tough big brother, eh?"

"I don't want to say it will pass. I don't think it ever will. But it will get easier to accept. Frank, you need to remind yourself that well over 300,000 made it out of Dunkirk. It won't minimise the losses, but it helps."

"See, that's why you're an officer, and I'm just a lance Corporal," Frank smiled as he took out two cigarettes. "We can finish these, and then I'll report in."

It started to rain again as Ian slowly walked home. He hadn't and wouldn't say anything to anybody about what Frank had told him. It upset him knowing how much his brother was suffering, but he couldn't tell his mum or dad.

Everyone was celebrating the achievements of the navy and the civilian armada that evacuated so many troops. Still, very few wanted to discuss the tens of thousands of Commonwealth and French soldiers left behind. Ian walked into the kitchen where his mother was sitting with a telegram lying face down in front of her.

"It's for you, son."

He had expected word from Major Hughes telling him to report back to his old Barracks, not to meet at Paddington Station. Although he could not see her, Ian could sense his mother's eyes staring at him.

"I had better pack. I've got to catch the overnight train to London."

"Tonight?"

"Yeah."

"I met Sadie O'Connor at the grocer's. Her son is still missing somewhere in Belgium." Peggy started to cry, and Ian held his mum as she quietly sobbed. "Do you think this damned war will be over soon?"

"I don't know, mum. I really don't know."

Ian selected his seat, hoping his carriage would be quiet. Leaving his jacket and bag on the seat, he stepped off the train to stand a little longer with his parents on the platform. He had told them not to come out to see him off, but they insisted. The platform was getting busier, with troops making their own way back to the Regimental Barracks.

"Take these sandwiches. They'll keep you going until you get to London," his mum said with a teary smile.

"Thanks, mum. I'll write as soon as I know where I've been stationed."

His dad passed him a brown paper bag with four cans of beer and a quarter bottle of whiskey. "That might help you get a sleep."

The whistle blasted for everyone to board as the train was ready to leave. All down the length of the platform, people were embracing and kissing, many in tears. Ian hugged and kissed his mum, feeling her tears running down her cheeks. His dad pulled him in close. "Take care and write when you can."

Ian climbed on the train, surprised to see his carriage was still empty, although that did not last long as four young lads from the Royal Artillery Corp. slid the door open and came in.

"Evening, Lieutenant. Are these seats free?"

"Help yourself."

"We are heading back to our depot. What about you, Sir?"

Ian had to think about that. The telegraph from Major Hughes was vague on where he would be stationed. "I'm not exactly sure where I will be posted. My company had been set up specifically for the campaign in Norway, but with that over, at least for now, I could be posted anywhere."

"I bet it was bloody cold in Norway."

"Yeah, it definitely was," Ian replied, thinking of the hours lying on the ledge freezing to death.

"We have just finished basic training. The course was cut short to build up the Corp's numbers. The Regiment suffered major losses in Belgium and Dunkirk."

"I am going to have a couple of drinks, then try and get some shut-eye. I have four cans of beer and a wee dram. I'm happy to share."

"No, you keep them, Lieutenant. We brought enough for ourselves. But don't worry, we will keep the noise down when you're sleeping."

"Thanks, lads."

Chapter 6

As Ian stepped off the train, he saw Andrew Hughes right away.

"How was your trip?"

"Fine, I managed to get a sleep, but I'd like to go somewhere to have a wash and change my shirt."

"No problem. Do you want some breakfast first? The station canteen is open?"

"That sounds great."

The two men sat talking about what they had been up to over the last couple of days. Andrew then explained, why Paddington Station, telling him where they were meeting the Brigadier.

"Baker Street?"

"64 Baker Street, it's very near."

When they arrived at number 64, the Brigadier and another person were waiting for them. Andrew stuck out his hand and started to introduce himself and Ian.

"Let's just leave the introductions out," the stranger said.

Ian looked from Andrew to the Brigadier, then back to the stranger.

"I want to be perfectly clear; this meeting never occurred, and everything said here has the highest top secret rating. Is that understood?"

Andrew looked at the Brigadier, and he nodded. "Understood,"

"And you?" the stranger said, staring at Ian.

"Understood."

"I know you are just back from Norway, and here as a country, we are frantically trying to regroup our defences. At the same time trying to reassure the public that we are prepared for any Nazi invasion. Our Home Guard has been mobilised, and people's awareness has been aroused. I understand Major, that you are aware of our plans to establish a special non-military Auxiliary Unit loosely regarded as part of the Home Guard but effectively very separate. For now, I shall leave the details of the actual role and training of the Auxiliaries and address our main concern. Have either of you heard of the Brandenburgers?"

Both men shook their heads.

"They are the brainchild of one Hauptmann von Hippel. A German Intelligence officer we have been watching for some time now. In brief, he had proposed sending troops dressed as civilian workers into countries the Wehrmacht planned to invade, Poland, Denmark, and Norway. Their role would be to secure and protect strategic targets to assist the troops during their invasion or sabotage any structures the defenders needed to repel the invasion. The Wehrmacht rejected his proposal out of hand. So, he took the proposal to Admiral Wilhelm Canaris, the head of the Abwehr, German Military Intelligence. Unlike the officers of the Wehrmacht, Canaris was neither shocked nor appalled by the proposal. He convinced Hitler, who authorised the tactic. Canaris's only concern was that von Hippel may unintentionally expose his three-year covert operation in Britain."

"You're saying you believe they are already here?" Ian asked.

"We know Canaris has agents in Britain because we have already caught some. What we don't know is how many and where they might be operating."

Brigadier Gubbins stood up and slowly paced the office before speaking. "Andrew, you knew I worked for Military Intelligence before heading up four of the Independent Companies. What you did not know was my overriding role there. If we could hold Norway, we were to. If not, we were to identify troops and civilians that we could train and put back as saboteurs to wreak havoc on the German occupiers. Before going to Norway and since my return, I have had a team of MI(R) agents working around the clock to identify vulnerable locations. Places we would install people if it was our campaign. We have identified about thirty main locations, and these are the areas we plan to insert our special units."

Andrew and Ian sat listening to the operation's overview. They were surprised to hear how advanced the plans were. Even to the extent that secret underground bunkers were being installed by a special engineering squad. These forces were now absorbed by MI(R) and would not be returning to their regiment. Brigadier Gubbins told them that he planned to take them on a site inspection tomorrow.

"who or what is MI(R)?" asked Andrew.

"Military Intelligence Research," replied Gubbins.

"I have a question," Ian said.

"Go ahead, ask."

"Why am I part of this operation. I mean, I am a Lieutenant from a territorial company who was sent to Norway, not a spy?"

"Shall I answer that, Brigadier?"

"Yes, go right ahead."

"That is precisely why you and Major Hughes have been selected to oversee the special unit. We are concerned that the Abwehr may have a sleeper within our Intelligence operation, and this is too critical to take the risk, hence meeting in this building. And with that, I think I'll leave you."

"Well lads, we have plans to sort out, but first, a spot of lunch and a drink is in order."

"One drink," Andrew said with a smile.

"We'll see," laughed the Brigadier.

Chapter 7

The next three weeks flew in. Andrew and Ian were shown a wholly, secret, paramilitary operation from numerous offices with obscure business names in London. They were also taken to newly acquired manner houses where scientists and engineers planned, designed, built, and tested new explosive devices. Some of the devices were unimaginable to Andrew and Ian. They were shown a range of unique, small bombs, activated by different kinds of detonators, such as the acid pencil or pressure detonator. One of these small explosive devices was aptly called, "the castrator." The explosive was activated when a person stepped on the pressure switch.

Driving south-eastwards from London, they met the Brigadier in the town of Ashford in Kent. The party then made their way, less than a mile south, to one of the first built Auxiliary bunkers.

It was explained to them there would be several, separately run, operations. These Auxiliary operations, nick-named 'Scallywag Saboteurs,' would remain separate from the Home Guard. The Brigadier explained the tiered levels of secret communications, and, how intelligence gathered by civilian-trained spies part of his Special Duties Branch, would stay behind should the invasion occur. Their role was strictly limited to gathering intelligence which they would drop off at agreed, disguised pick-up areas. From there, runners would pass the messages on to Out Stations where wireless sets were innovatively concealed, some in hay lofts, some in church pulpits or in the local tavern's cellars. If the OUT Stations were discovered or too dangerous to be used, the regular army would rely on the final tier, the IN Stations. These were further back, more centralised, and more extensive underground bunkers. Unlike the field bunkers designed for short stays, these bunkers were designed for wireless operators to stay hidden and keep transmitting until relieved or captured.

"I am confused. I thought the Auxiliaries were a single operation designed to disrupt, the German occupying forces, through acts of sabotage. Now you're saying there are a Special Duties Branch whose sole role is to gather and pass on intelligence information," Andrew said.

"I was of the same opinion, Sir," Ian reiterated.

"Our preparations are multi-tiered. It's a bit difficult to explain but let me try."

The Brigadier went on to outline the various overlapping roles. The Home Guard come under the army's jurisdiction. They will take over some of the regular army's duties, freeing them to train thousands of new recruits. Then there's both the Domestic Secret Service MI5 and External Secret Intelligence Service MI6, who are working closely with Special Branch on counter-espionage areas.

I will run several other operations, ranging from Weapon Research Units, Propaganda Warfare Teams, Auxiliary intelligence Special Duties and Auxiliary Field Patrols, so called, Scallywags to carry out sabotage and, if necessary, assassinations.

"So, hopefully, now you can understand why I need you both to oversee the Field Patrols training. Oh, and just to add to that, Churchill wants me to plan and oversee the new Commandos training program in Scotland," Brigadier Gubbins said.

"Is that all?" laughed Andrew.

"I am scared to look in my inbox tray in the morning; in case they have more projects for me to oversee."

Once back in London, the three men agreed to meet later that night for dinner and to further discuss the best way forward.

"I'll see you both later," said the Brigadier.

"Do you want to go for a beer?" Andrew asked Ian.

"Definitely."

"Do you think the Brigadier looks done in?" asked Andrew.

"I do, but I'm not surprised given his workload. I had planned to tell him I wanted to be assigned to the new Commando Company, but now…" Ian said.

"I know, and just to let you know, I have already discussed this with him. He understands our position but has asked, not ordered, us to help him. Christ, he's already up to his eyes with issues."

"I suppose we have little choice but to stay and get the training regime established. But once it's up and running, I will be asking for a transfer," Ian said.

"Me too."

Chapter 8

The training for the selected Auxiliary candidates took place at Coleshill. Both Andrew and Ian were hands-on instructors. Their understanding from their briefing by MI6 intelligence officer, Peter Fleming, they would have to train between 1,000 and 3,000 volunteers to adequately cover the extensive invasion area. Although both Scotland's East and West coasts had identified landing areas, the vast majority were in the southwest of England. The whole coastline of the southeast was peppered with Auxiliary Patrol units. A special Royal Engineers unit attached to the Brigadier's operation had installed hundreds of small secret underground bunkers. Basically, the bunkers were a version of the Anderson Shelters with a hidden entrance and an escape tunnel should the enemy find the door. After Ian inspected the bunkers, he made a few suggestions for added security. The three main ones being, firstly the need for the entry ladder to go 18 inches below the bunker floor level. His rationale was that if the enemy found the entrance and dropped a grenade down the shaft, it would be below the floor level and could contain the shrapnel. His second suggestion was to narrow the underground entrance, that would impede pursuers, buying time to escape down the tunnel. The wall, making the entry narrower, must also be blast-proof, and lastly, a bolted door closing off the tunnel from inside the tunnel. The Engineer officer in charge was visibly annoyed when he was ordered to retrofit already constructed bunkers.

Andrew walked into the office just as the argument finished. The engineers officer stormed out, leaving Ian standing holding drawings.

"He seemed rather annoyed," Ian said.

"Captains don't like taking orders from lowly lieutenants. But fuck him, these alterations could mean the difference between life and death to our volunteers. Anyway, how are the volunteers holding up?"

"It's complex. You have your gamekeeper and poacher. They can move silently, and both can, under the right circumstances, kill. However, they are hopeless at wireless operating, map-reading, and being subtle. Then there are your doctors, dentists, school teachers, white collar professionals. They understand the intelligence objectives and can operate the wireless, but they can't gut a dead rabbit without throwing up. And lastly, there are the Nazi haters, often quite smart and capable, but they tend to overestimate their skills and put their unit in danger."

"That sounds like nothing you can't handle," Andrew smiled.

"What do you know about these field security police?"

"I know they have been re-named to Field Security Service, FSS. Why?"

"They are all non-commissioned officers, but they seem to have a fair amount of power, considering their rank. And I spoke to one of them yesterday, a corporal, and got the impression their designated rank is meaningless."

"They are part of the reformed Army Intelligence Corp disbanded shortly after World War One. And three of the 36 sections in total will be working for us under the Brigadier's Command."

"Doing what?" Ian asked.

"That varies depending on which section they are from. Some will have the role of ensuring our various training facilities' security, and cover story is watertight. They will also covertly check out the local communities and determine if there are any security risks that need to be addressed. Others, within the sections have been chosen for their language skills and will be placed with our exiled recruits."

"Are we going to be training those exiled troops as well?"

"That is the plan."

Over the next few months, Andrew travelled extensively between the Scottish Highlands and Dover, spending most of his time in the southwest of England. While Ian spent his days at the training camp at Coleshill House.

The volunteers trained as units of four. And although they all had training in each aspect of their duties, each unit had a dedicated wireless and morse code operator, a first aid field medic, an explosive expert, and a sniper. These volunteers were placed with regular trainers from the respective regular army regiments.

Andrew knew an number of other officers, working for the Brigadier, had identified more than thirty possible target areas, mainly, but not exclusively, from Margate to Bournemouth, and inland from Salisbury to Canterbury. The Brigadier had plans for two hundred, independent Auxiliary field units, made up of four to eight operatives within that sector alone.

On July 10th the Battle for Britain commenced. The whole country were in awe of the RAF fighter pilots, though outnumbered, their resilience, skill, and bravery shocked and stunned the Luftwaffe command. Then, mid-way through this battle, on August 24^{th,} 1940, a single German bomber, whether by accident or not, dropped the first bomb on London City. Churchill was furious and ordered a bombing raid on Berlin. Then Hitler, in a wild rant, ordered a Blitz on London. And an over enthusiastic Luftwaffe further targeted and bombed other strategic cities throughout Britain.

As the Blitz intensified, Churchill and his War Cabinet demanded daily reports of the country's readiness to repel a German invasion. He knew the Royal Airforce were inflicting heavy losses on the German Luftwaffe. And ordered the Royal Navy to sacrifice other areas to ensure they maintained superiority in the English Channel and the North Sea. But Churchill knew they still had to plan for a Blitzkrieg attack. Even with the Royal Navy voicing their confidence that they could maintain dominance over the English Channel, there were no guarantees that sufficient numbers of German landing crafts could not make the less than 20 miles crossing. Landing at a number of poorly defended coastal towns and swiftly linking up with their advanced Blitzkrieg paratroopers.

Hugh Dalton, the Minister responsible for the newly formed Minister of Economic Warfare, Brigadier Gibbins's superior, called him to a meeting to discuss future projects.

"Come in Colin. Would you like a drink?"

"Only on days ending in Y," he smiled.

"Ever since this bloody bombing started, Winston has been on the warpath. He wants you to rapidly expand and train more Commando units. And I want you to put Major Hughes and Lieutenant Anderson in charge, to oversee the training at Arisaig, on the West coast of Scotland."

"Arisaig?"

"It's one of our newly acquired remote estates, just west of Fort William."

"What about the Auxiliaries and their training?"

"I think the training can be managed fine with the current team at Coleshill, minus Hughes and Anderson."

Dolton sipped his drink before continuing. "Winston also wants you to establish a special force to operate as saboteurs behind enemy lines."

"As spies?"

"No, that's MI6's area. And, they are not happy with Winston's proposal, but he made it clear it will happen."

"Why are we doubling up training Commandos and Agents?"

"Although much of the training will be the same and take place at the same facilities, our commandos are part of the army and will fight under army jurisdiction and as uniformed troops.

The other agents will be part of Special Operations Executive and under your command doing Winston's bidding."

"Which is what exactly?"

"Quite simply, to set Europe ablaze."

Chapter 9

Ian was glad to hear that he was being redeployed to Scotland. He had been happy enough at Coleshill but for some time now, felt he could easily leave the base, and it would run smoothly. Andrew had also asked him to review all the Auxiliaries they had trained to see if there were suitable candidates who could be trained to qualify as Special Operations Executive agents. The prerequisite was, firstly, a reasonable level of fitness, which would be enhanced by the time they've finished their training in Scotland. But more importantly, these candidates must speak at least one European language, and at this point, preferably French.

Andrew knew all the candidates would have achieved a reasonable competence in wireless operations and basic sabotage techniques at Coleshill, but none had undergone hand-to-hand combat training.

Having been close to the Auxiliary recruits Ian knew the language requirement would take out ninety per cent of the existing Auxiliaries. As he worked his way through every personal file shortlisting the potential candidates and reviewing their attributes, a glaring omission jumped out at him.

Ian knew he had better meet with Andrew and the Brigadier.

Andrew, wanting to hear what Ian's concerns were, arranged for them to meet in London the following day.

"Ian, how are you doing?" asked the Brigadier.

"Fine, Sir."

"While we are in a bar having a drink, Ian, it's Colin, okay?"

"Yes, Colin."

"I've never been here, and to tell the truth, I thought you were joking about meeting here." Major Hughes said.

"Well, Andrew the office in Baker Street is getting pretty crowded with all the coming and going. So, I thought, let's meet at the Sherlock

Homes pub. I am a big fan of Sir Arthur Conan Doyle and always make it a point to have a drink here every time I am in London."

"So, what's troubling you Ian?" Andrew asked.

"Well," Ian paused then pulled out his notebook.

"I have drawn up the list, within the parameters you required, mainly looking for language skills. And none of the potential candidates with language skills were trained, at our sniper training range."

"What's that got to do with it?" Andrew asked.

"We only sent those recruits that we believed could, if necessary, kill someone, for sniper training. As part of my assessment of which Auxiliaries would be suitable for further training, I gauged their skills and temperament against a range of scenarios. One of the scenarios was the potential necessity to kill up close and in cold blood. None of the selected candidates, the ones with the language skills, could in my opinion shoot someone, let alone use a knife to kill an unsuspecting target."

Colin picked up his drink and then looked at Ian.

"If you had been asked two years ago if you could kill someone in cold blood, are you sure you could have answered that same scenario positively?"

"No."

"Then let's get them to Scotland and let Fairbairn and Sykes train them."

"Who?" Asked Ian.

"Two very interesting characters. One an ex-Shanghai copper and the other the finest marksman I have ever seen with any pistol, rifle or machine gun. They will be training both the SOE agents and the newly formed Commando companies in unconventional firearms techniques and street fighting unarmed combat."

"Don't we have army instructors already earmarked for hand-to-hand combat training?"

"Not like these two, you don't."

"If I may?"

"What's on your mind Ian?"

"As I understand it, these SOE agents will be doing the same training as our commando units in the West of Scotland."

"That's correct," agreed Andrew. "Then they will do parachute training at Ringway, and spy trade craft training at Beaulieu, what we call our finishing school. All up, the training will run three months."

"I am not sure how many recruits you will require to go through the training," said Ian. "So, my request is that I be allowed to transfer into one of the newly formed Commando Units. And then, if and when required, be seconded back to assist with establishing and training SOE agents. Whilst at the same time being able to take part in any scheduled Commando operations assigned to my company. As per our previous agreement."

"I accept my previous commitment to you, and in light of that, can agree, with some limitations," Colin replied.

"What do you mean, limitations?" Asked Ian.

"I will arrange for you to be transferred to Lovat's Scouts, soon to form No4 Commando Company. Of course, you will have to do all the unit's training. I know Simon, Lord Lovat well. He and his cousin David Stirling have raised the proposition of forming an unorthodox group of shock fighters. A Special Commando Air Service. I will speak with him and explain our unique requirements. But let me be clear on this point, you are more valuable to your country training SOE agents to fight and survive behind enemy lines than as an, all be it, courageous commando."

"Well, I," Andrew said. But the Brigadier cut him off.

"I know what I promised you both, and I feel particularly bad. But Andrew, I will need you to run our field SOE agents."

Andrew, clearly unhappy, reluctantly accepted what was to be his future. "Well at least I insist on doing the full training program, including the parachute training that all SOE agents must do."

Colin nodded his approval.

"Okay, Ian, it's between you and Colin here to buy all the drinks tonight. I am paying for sod all," Andrew said, with a grin.

Chapter 10

In preparation for the SOE training, every instructor had to complete the scheduled course twice before they were able to offer suggested amendments to the course.

Now it was Andrew and Ian to test what the instructors had settled on as the agreed course. Both men privately felt confident that they had adequately prepared for the sabotage exercise.

Both had found the course very stretching and now found themselves tasked with the final assignment. On a bleak moor in the wilds of Scotland's West Coast Highlands. The temperature plummeted as the small group of men lay shivering at the mouth of a shallow cave. With numb fingers, they cleaned their Thompson sub-machine guns, meticulously drying them and finally adding a light drop of oil. Once the weapons were sorted out and after a final check of each operatives' explosives and detonators the team were ready. They decided to eat the last of their rations and then rest before the final push. One of the group took the first two-hour watch while the others huddled together trying to share body heat.

"Did I really agree to do the full training course?" Andrew asked.

'No, you didn't agree. You insisted on doing it," Ian said.

"Well, next time I insist on doing special training, kick me under the table."

As a group they lay down at the back of the cave out of the swirling wind and tried to sleep.

Six hours later and still unimaginably cold, they started to make their way down the mountainside by the light of the full moon to the edge of the Loch. No one needed to speak, they just started stripping off all their clothes and placing them in oil-coated sacks. Then slowly, painfully, they entered the mirror-like Loch.

"Jesus Christ, it's freezing."

"Keep it down," Andrew said to the Sergeant.

The four-man team knew they would have to keep together as they, part swam part floated, across Loch Shiel. The group had been dropped off by boat at Inversanda on the westerly shore of Loch Linnhe. Crossing the country heading west to Strontian, then northwest to Pollock, near Loch Sheil. Their mission was to lay the charges that would destroy Glenfinnan Viaduct and then make their way to a rendezvous pick-up at Lochailort. Intelligence, already supplied, clearly showed the only way they could get onto the viaduct, without being spotted, was to approach from the west. That meant they would have to swim Loch Sheil at night. And although not told, they knew there would be numerous patrols searching for them along both sides of the Loch and blocking the only road from the east that they could take, to the viaduct.

Three-quarter of the way across the Loch, Andrew let out a cry, lost grip of his bag, and slid under the water. Ian shoved his sack to one of the others, then ducked under the water, grabbing Andrew, and pulling him to the surface. The other two in the group pulled both men to them. Andrew, his face was contorted in pain signalled that he was okay.

When they eventually reached the other side of the Loch, they all quickly helped Andrew get into his dry clothes. As soon as they were all dressed Ian checked Andrew. His core temperature had dropped, and Ian, from past personal knowledge, knew Andrew needed to have his core temperature raised somehow. Ian and the Sergeant went looking for a sheltered spot, it needed to be somewhere where they could light a fire without giving their position away. They found a hillside overhang which gave partial cover above and on three sides. Luckily, they were able to find dead, dry branches which would burn without too much smoke. Ian knew he had to act quickly, they had to take the chance of capture. He rigged up netting to cover the opening and lit a small fire.

"Ian, you three should press on while it's still dark," Andrew stated.

"No we need to finish this as a team," replied Ian.

"No, Ian, we don't. Our objective is to lay the charges sufficiently to completely destroy the viaduct within the scheduled time, and I will not have us fail."

"But."

"But nothing. You must complete the mission and make it to the escape rendezvous point. I will head straight there after I have rested."

"What about the hunter patrols?"

"I'll take my chances, and if they spot me, it might pull them away from you. Now go. You still have time to complete the mission."

It was agreed to take all the packs and only leave Andrew to carry his Thompson sub-machine gun and sidearm.

Half an hour after the others had left, and feeling much better, Andrew put out the fire, removed the netting and headed north towards the road leading to Lochailort. The plan had required them to plant their explosives and then make the twenty-five miles to the pick-up before the charges exploded. The last part of the exercise would leave them exposed, and they had to complete the mission before daylight. They all knew the only way they could successfully complete the task and reach the rendezvous was to attack from the west.

The team had studied the viaducts' structure and knew exactly where to place their explosives. They had practiced numerous times, fixing their shaped explosives on a simulated model, determining the optimum stress points to ensure maximum destruction. When they reached the viaduct, they split three ways and went to work silently, placing the explosives at all the stress sections.

The plan had been for Andrew to take up a covering position to warn the others if a patrol was above them, and to give cover fire if everything went wrong. Now they had the added pressure of keeping their own watch as they laid their charges.

It was nearly four-thirty am when all the charges and detonators were in place. The three-men regrouped and started to slip away from the bridge, just as a guard patrol arrived.

"Take cover, and don't move," whispered Ian.

Our pick-up will leave if we don't get to the rendezvous before daylight, and that's not looking good. he thought.

Ian knew if they missed that pick-up, they would have to evade hunters for another twenty-four hours until they could meet at their backup rendezvous.

It was still dark at six o'clock when the guards moved back across the viaduct. No one said anything, but they all knew there was little chance of reaching their pick-up point.

"Right, lads, I don't need to state the obvious about our chances of making the pick-up, but we have to make as much distance from here before the shit hits the fan."

After running hard for an hour and exhausted, they stopped, desperately needing a rest.

"I don't think we have a cat's chance in hell of making our rendezvous before daylight,"

"We have to try. Let's move," Ian ordered the others, even though he knew the Sergeant was right.

Just then an old farm truck pulled out from a forest clearing. They were just about to dive to the ground when Ian saw Andrew waving to them.

"Come on, hurry up. We can still make it."

Later, back at base, exhausted, but elated, it was accepted that the mission had been a success. The viaduct would have been destroyed, and the team would have got away.

Chapter 11

Back in London, Andrew had arranged for the first group of candidates from the Auxiliaries to commence their paramilitary guerrilla warfare training at Arisaig before sending them to Ringway for parachute training. And, finally, to Beaulieu in the New Forest, for spy trade craft training.

On the groups arrival in Scotland, Ian was there to meet them. He told them they were about to go through the most intensive training any troops have ever had. And warned them that if they were not prepared to give one hundred per cent, now was their last chance to leave, and not to even bother unpacking their kit. No one took up his offer to leave.

He told them. "By the time your training is finished, you will be at your fittest, be an excellent map reader, an accomplished explosive saboteur and able to silently kill."

Ian knew, even after going through the training program, some candidates wouldn't make it. What the recruits did not know was that to avoid any security risk, failed or dropped out recruits would be sent to a holding camp, nick named, the Cooler, at Inverlair.

First, there was the gruelling physical slog over the harshest of terrain that the instructors could find. No candidate survived that without numerous cuts and bruises. Then, there was the capture and evasion exercise, followed by weapon training, firing everything from a Colt 45 to the Sten gun and their favourite Thompson sub-machine gun. Generally agreed to be the favourite sub-machine gun available. Rather than teaching the recruits to aim, the instructors taught them to tuck their firing arm into their hip, point their body at their target, and fire two quick shots, known as a double tap.

With the cooperation of the West Highland local railway line, the recruits were taught how and where to plant explosives to destroy tracks, bridges, and train engines.

The other main training session, and all said, the most challenging, was the hand-to-hand combat, silent killing training. Brigadier Gubbins had secured the services of William (Bill) Fairbairn and Eric Sykes. Fairbairn an ex-Shanghai police detective, and Sykes a firearms agent, considered to be one of the world's top marksmen, to train the recruits. They had designed a unique stiletto double-bladed fighting knife which would be issued to every SOE agent and British Commando, as essential kit.

"Listen up," bellowed Bill Fairbairn. "What you will be taught by Eric and me is dirty, brutal, and barbaric, but if you need to do it, it will save your life. This knife, holding up their invention, is designed for one thing and one thing only. To kill your enemy before he kills you. Eric."

"Thanks Bill. You have to clear, from your mind, any notion of fairness or Queensberry Rules. It's survival. It has to be brutal, and it has to be quick." Eric looked at the stunned group.

He continued. "Your rib cage is well designed to protect vital organs from things bashing into them. It's like body armour for a knife striking downwards, but it's useless against a knife thrusting upwards. And while I am at it, not all organs are protected."

Everyone simultaneously looked at their groin.

"The only time I want to see your knife higher than your waist is when you stick it in your target's neck."

One of the recruits rushed out of the room and just made it outside before he threw up.

Ian wouldn't actually run any of the training sessions. He had been given oversite of the training, for agent who would operate in France and Norway. He decided, as part of his commitment to them, to participate in the more arduous parts of the course.

However, his role at Arisaig, was not only to assess the recruits but also the instructors. He had watched their different techniques. How some instructors simply drove recruits hard to dropping point. Others, while still driving them hard, brought out the best in the recruits by encouraging, and motivating them.

Ian knew there was a place for both styles of training. The hard-line instructors were best suited for early selection phase, weeding out the recruits who would struggle with isolation in the field. While the other style was better suited to recruits once they had crossed the physical fitness threshold, where the training, though still very difficult, was also about building technical skills.

On the last day, after the completion of the training program, on the last day, Ian would sit with all the instructors. During the training he'd been supplied with regular ongoing assessments from all the instructors. And, now it was the time to assess each recruit's strengths and weaknesses. In the last group the reports had highlighted the fact that three recruits had dropped out, before the hand-to-hand combat training, and another four during that training. These seven had been sent to the quarantine camp, the Cooler.

"So, we have twenty-three left out of the original thirty successful candidates. All have achieved various levels of skills. But from your reports some concerns still remain. So, do we pass them all onto Ringway, or send some to the Cooler?" Ian asked.

It was Bill Fairbairn who spoke first. "I am worried about two candidates. Henry, the quietly spoken lad and Sharon, the teacher."

"They are excellent recruits," another instructor said.

"I know, and they're probably the smartest in the group. But I don't think they could kill in cold blood."

"Bill, right from the start of this program I had doubts as to whether a civilised human could kill in cold blood. I still have those doubts, but I don't think we can ever know for sure until they are faced with a life-or-death situation," Ian said.

"I agree, and for that reason, I am happy to pass them on to Ringway. But before they are sent on any mission, you need to be aware of their possible limitations, and, you, would need to reinforce to them that other lives could depend on them being able to silently kill the enemy."

Ian then asked every instructor, individually, if they had any other comments, or concerns? But they simply agreed that Bill had sufficiently covered their concerns.

As agreed, Ian followed the twenty-three to Ringway, and watched them all going from shivering jellies, before their first jump.,to hyped-up adrenaline seekers wanting to jump again and again.

He was encouraged to see that day by day, the recruits were growing with confidence, and they were now ready for their final training at Beaulieu. Here, they were taught personal security, what clothes to wear, briefed on the location and documents they would carry, checking their accents and skills at communications in the field, using codes and drop-offs, and covert propaganda. They were also taught how to act under police surveillance. Next, was instructions on how to carry out a burglary, lock picking, and how to quickly disguise yourself with simple props, easy to conceal. And, instructed on how to make secret contacts and tail someone without being spotted.

Lastly, they were told they would be given two sets of pills if or when they went on a mission. Benzedrine to keep you awake and the other 'L' tablet, which came in a little rubber cover. The suicide pill, which, when bitten, would kill them within 15 seconds.

After completing their training at Beaulieu the candidates were sent back to their auxiliary unit, to wait for further orders.

As agreed, Ian was assigned, and told to report to, Lord Lovat's No. 4 Commando Unit.

Chapter 12

"So, you're the new chap, here to show us how it's all done?" said the Captain, staring at Ian.

"Ian Anderson."

"Yes. Simon Frazer."

"Lord Lovat?" Ian asked.

"Well, that's the title, but I am Captain Simon Frazer, or simply, Shimi, to my friends."

At first, Lovat and his men, formally Lovat's Scouts and now the newly formed No 4 Commando, were sceptical about Ian. They had trained together as Territorials before signing up as regulars and had built their own esprit de corps. But within two days of training with Ian leading from the front, he was brought into their fold.

It had proven to be one of the worst winters in years as No 4 Commando was put through its training. Constantly wet, cold, and sore, they exercised on the moors.

At the end of their training everyone was given a weeks, leave except Ian, who was told he had to report to London.

"No rest for you over Christmas, Ian? "Lovat asked.

"I hope to get home for Christmas before my next cohort at Arisaig starts training."

"When will you join us next, or is that a secret?"

"Brigadier Gubbins wants me to oversee the next group of trainees, then to conduct inspections of, well, I can't really say what. But I should be back with the Company in mid to late February unless the Company is to be deployed. If those orders come through, I will be back sooner."

"You know Gubbins wants you back full-time and hopes this posting proves unworkable?"

"I will just have to prove him wrong," Ian smiled.

"I'm sure you will. Anyway, I hope you manage to have some time at home over Christmas, because next year will be full on."

On arriving back in London Ian caught up with Andrew Hughes the night before they were both scheduled to meet Brigadier Gubbins.

He gave Andrew an overview of how the SOE training for his sector was proceeding and then about his deployment with Lovat's Company.

As they walked towards Covent Garden. Andrew stopped as they were about to enter the famous Punch and Judy Pub. Pulling Ian to the side.

"It's noisy in there. So, before we go in, I need to tell you why I wanted to meet with you tonight."

"What's on the Brigadier's mind?" Ian asked.

"He wants you back full-time. And he will argue that you are much more valuable to train and mentor agents. And I hate to say this, but he's right."

Ian said nothing, turned from the pub and started to walk away from Andrew towards Piccadilly Circus. He knew it was not Andrew's decision but still he felt betrayed by them both.

Andrew caught up with him, and the two men walked in silence for five minutes. Then Ian abruptly stopped and turned to his friend.

"He either accepts the arrangement, or I am out. I mean that."

Both men stared at each other.

"I really mean that," Ian said in a more subdued tone.

"I know you do. Don't attend tomorrow's 9 am meeting. Go straight to the Baker Street office instead. I'll meet Colin at 9.00 and tell him we caught up last night for a couple of drinks. And I will let him know you want to be permanently transferred to Lovat's company, and you believe you can fulfil both duties. He won't like it, but I think I will be able to get it over the line."

"Thanks, Andrew."

"Now, let's get in somewhere warm and have a drink."

Next morning the three men met at the Baker Street office just before lunch; After pleasantries, and before Andrew laid out the training schedule for the next year, the Brigadier acknowledged Ian's position and accepted his proposal to stay with Lovat's Commando unit and participate in missions. With the proviso that it must fit in with Andrew's critical program.

"From now on, we will set up country operational sections. F section will send their first agents into Vichy, France, to start building contact cells. This group will be our test dummies to see if we have the right paperwork and cover stories. If we have serious gaps in our preparation I would rather find that out with agents operating in Vichy, than occupied France. Shortly after that, and if we are satisfied with our preparation, we will send our first units into occupied France then Norway. The first groups will be in March next year. After our agents are settled, and communications are up and running, we will start organising and training resistance teams. Initially, we will be training local resistance members as radio operators only. Sabotage training will come later. Each sector will be structured around its own adapted Auxiliary style cells.

"Ian, I want you involved in all the F section field agent selections. You have trained with the current Auxiliary agents and are best placed to give the final sign-off on who to deploy."

Ian nodded. "When do you want me to report?"

"As I said we start selection on 6 January, with the first deployment to Vichy, France. Then in late February or early March. Our first group of agents will be dropped behind enemy lines in both France and Norway by late March or early April," Andrew said. "Brigadier, do you have anything to add?"

"No, Andrew I think you've covered everything for now. I want to thank you both for everything you have achieved in these past months. And while it's been tough, next year will be far more challenging. So, please try and enjoy some time with your families."

The Brigadier left Andrew to finalise January's meetings.

"How did he take my wanting to stay with No 4 Company?"

"Better than expected. Although he is considering another posting, rather than Lovat's Commandos."

"What do you mean by another posting.

"Do you know Davis Stirling?"

"No."

"He's Lovat's cousin and he is arguing for a military special saboteur unit. He's calling it the Special Air Brigade, and he is gaining support from senior army generals. Colin wants to do the right thing by you. He's a good commanding officer."

"I know, and thanks again," Ian said.

"What are your plans for the rest of the day?"

"If I rush, I can catch the afternoon train to Glasgow."

"Well, get moving man, don't keep your mum waiting."

Chapter 13

Ian arrived home to find his mum in the kitchen peeling potatoes. She always made her own potato scones for Christmas morning's breakfast.

"Hi, mum."

"Ian, I didn't know you were coming home," she said with a happy tear in her eye.

"Neither did I until very recently. Is Frank still in the barracks?"

"No, Frank's battalion has just recently been deployed to Egypt. He says he is part of the Western Desert Force, whatever that is."

"And dad?"

"He's working. He will be so glad to hear your home. How long will you be able to stay?"

"I hope, if nothing changes, to get about ten days before I take up my new post."

"Where will you be posted, son?"

"Sorry, Mum, I can't tell you."

"That's okay son. Take your dad for a pint when he comes home that will give me some peace and quiet to get things ready for Christmas."

"What about you. Don't you want to join us?"

"I've got too much to do, but you can bring me back something to celebrate you're being home."

Ian gave his mum a kiss. He was determined to make this Christmas as special as he could for his mum and dad because things were going to get a lot worse before they got better.

After his Christmas break, Ian, back at Arisaig, reviewed the past SOE trained candidates. He now needed to concentrate on those most proficient in French and Norwegian who could blend in easily. This was greatly helped by the fact he had trained exiled forces from both countries, but he knew he would also have to send in British trained agents. Next, he considered their main activities and determined they needed excellent communications skills and an ability to train and lead resistant fighters.

Turning his mind to the two, though similar, different risks faced by these agents. He split his F section into two groups. The first group destined for Vichy France had to meet every point identified in his selection criteria. The second group, selected for operating in occupied France, would not only need to be proficient, they needed to excel, they also had to be the best candidates.

Looking at the photographs in the files, he recognised most of their faces, but their names slipped his memory.

Ian then spent the next few meetings with the lead instructors and pondered over the strengths and weaknesses of each candidate before making his final selection.

There was a buzz of excitement in the air when the selected candidates arrived back at Arisaig. Ian gave them the now memorised induction. Alerted them to expectations they would have to meet and gave them one last chance to pull out and return to their unit. As usual, no one pulled out. This time they all made it through their refresher course except for two who were withdrawn days from completion due to climbing injuries. However, Ian assured them they would be written up as having passed the training, allowing them to join a future cohort when they recovered enough to complete their last two weeks at Beaulieu.

"Lieutenant Anderson," called the clerk leaning out the administration hut's window.

"Yes."

"It's a call from Captain Frazer."

Excitement exploded in Ian as he rushed into the room and picked up the phone.

"Sir."

"Ian, are you able to join the Company right now?"

"Yes, I have just finished the last training session."

"You need to grab your kit and meet me at Achnacarry. And I'll brief you on our way to Inveraray."

As the men headed southwards, Lord Lovat asked Ian if he had heard of Lofoten Island. Ian stated that all he knew of Lofoten was that the Island was in the northwest of Norway and had several fairly large fishing towns, but apart from that, nothing.

Lovat informed Ian that No 3 and No 4 Commando units were training for a raid on the Island's facilities. He explained the importance of the fish oil they produced for the German explosive factories. Their mission was to completely destroy the fish factories and blow up all the oil storage tanks. As an added bonus, one of the locals had passed on information that the German Commanding Officer's quarters also doubled as the local German Naval Headquarters.

"That's why I thought you would want to be involved in this operation. The problem, Ian, is I mentioned the operation to your Colonel Hughes, suggesting you take part in the raid. But he said you cannot be released for this mission. So, I need you to brief a selected snatch team on what intelligence they need to look for and gather."

"I need to get to London and sort this out."

"If you think you can get him to change his mind, go tonight."

"One way or another, I am going on the operation."

"I will make sure you're on tonight's train," Lovat said.

As soon as they arrived at Inveraray, Lovat arranged for transport to take Ian to Glasgow Central Station to catch that night's London train.

As the car pulled away, Ian saw Lovat's troops unloading assault landing crafts. He knew they would be training for the next four weeks, practising every aspect of the operation. Everyone knew speed would be critical for their success. The troops were also acutely aware of the perils of their up-and-coming sea voyage. Some knew that even after taking medication before joining their flotilla of navy destroyers, they were still likely to suffer seasickness. Still, even with that knowledge, every man was keen to be involved.

Before boarding the overnight train Ian arranged for a meeting with Andrew Hughes. At that meeting, the next day, Ian demanded to be allowed to be part of the raid.

"I can't approve of your involvement. We have other missions and more importantly for your team is the attack on the major electrical transformer station at Pessac, close to Bordeaux. If we knock that out, we can, if not cripple the U boats, severely limit their operations," Andrew said.

"We have already trained the team for that mission, and they are now going through further sabotage with Cecil Clarke at Brickendonbury Manor. I am no longer involved."

"We still need you here, as their section leader. At least until after the mission."

"Then I am demanding a transfer. I have overseen more than a hundred recruits being trained. I have finished selecting the agents for Vichy and Occupied France and Norway's insertions. At this point Arisaig doesn't need me. So, as per our agreement, I should be allowed to serve with Lovat. Otherwise, I'm finished, and I want out."

"Your current role is more important to the war effort than being part of a Commando raid. That's why I can't approve of you going on this raid?"

"This is more than a demolition raid. It's a mission within a mission."

"What?"

"Our Commando units are, quite frankly, brilliant as shock troops, but we are only just finding our feet in small strategic raiding parties. And I don't mean snatch and grab. I mean behind enemy lines raiding parties. I know, Shimi, sorry Lord Lovat and his cousin Colonel Stirling have been discussing the formation, under Stirling, of a Special Services Brigade. We could use this operation as a model for a shock and awe operation. And, as an intelligence gathering operation."

"What intelligence gathering are you talking about?"

Ian explained what he had been told by Lovat about the Naval Headquarters and about the chance of securing secret U-boat codes.

Andrew was furious that he had not been made aware of Operation Claymore.

"When will the bloody military start confiding in us?"

"This gives us the perfect opportunity to show that we can blend our special skills in a shared operation," Ian said.

Armed with this new intelligence information Andrew, reluctantly agreed for Ian to be involved in the operation.

Ian spent the next few weeks training a special snatch team for the mission. The overall plan involved the main forces attacking the four small fishing towns and the German garrisons stationed there. Destroying the factories and oil storage tanks and sinking German trawlers. Ian's snatch team would capture and secure the German Commanders office and Naval Headquarters, holding it until he arrived.

Initially, Ian would participate in a special Royal Navy boarding party, securing German Naval codes before sinking their ships.

On 1 March 1941. Five hundred combined troops, mainly No 3 and No 4 Commando, boarded the destroyers for their three-day sail cross from Scapa Flow on Scotland's Orkney Island to Lofoten Island off the northwest coast of Norway.

The flotilla arrived off the Lofoten Islands in the early hours of 4 March. The troops had four separate destinations earmarked for destruction. It was agreed later on, at the debriefing, the raid had proven to be a complete success. Operation Claymore had met with little resistance, even though there were a number of crack German troops there, who put up a spirited resistance. The Commandos successfully destroyed all eleven fish oil factories and storage tanks. Over 800,000 gallons of oil and Glycerine needed by the German's munitions factories were destroyed. Five ships were sunk. One hundred German troops were killed, and ninety-eight taken prisoner. They also brought back to Scotland three hundred and fifteen Norwegian volunteers to be trained in guerrilla warfare, knowing that once trained, they would be sent back on sabotage missions in the years ahead. Not only were the Commandos elated, but the general public also rejoiced in the operation's success. What the general public did not know was Ian's teams' success. His boarding parties had snatched codebooks, submarine despatches and logistics records. But the biggest prize was obtained from the raiding party, which boarded the trawler Kerbs and captured a set of rotor wheels for the German Navy's Enigma cypher machine and code books. With the rotors and codebooks Bletchley Park was now able to read German U-Boat messages.

At their next meeting in the Sherlock Holmes Pub, no one could have wiped the smile off Ian's face. When Brigadier Gubbins and Colonel Andrew Hughes sat down to hear Ian's report of the operation.

"This time, the drinks are on me," smiled Ian.

"I'll have a double Glenmorangie with my pint," Brigadier Gubbins said.

"Make that two," Andrew said.

Ian brought the drinks to their table, sat down and, lifting his glass, toasted the operation.

"Terrific job. Your boys have done very well. Churchill could not stop laughing when he heard about Lieutenant Wills's telegram that he sent to, A. Hitler in Berlin. What were his exact words, Andrew?" Gubbins asked.

Andrew thought for a second. "The telegram was addressed to A Hitler and read," *In your last speech, you said German troops would meet the British wherever they landed. Where were your troops?*

Gubbins smiled. "And no casualties on our side, Ian, is that right?" Gubbins asked.

"Only some minor injuries. We took them completely by surprise."

"Well, tell the men, Churchill loved it."

"And Bletchley, got all the Intel and the rotors?" Ian asked.

"They did and are meticulously going through everything you brought back. And now even better news, Hitler must send more and more troops to defend his coastal positions."

"Ian, I will need you to give me a detailed report on what worked well on the day. But more importantly, what didn't," Andrew said.

"I will, Colonel." Ian smiled.

"By the way, Churchill is beside himself, with the success of the Pessac raid. The damage to the electrical supply has effectively shut down numerous manufacturing factories, and more importantly forcing the U-Boat to be pulled out of the area. On top of that he is pleased as punch with Lovat's success in Norway, and your seizure of Enigma gear and German Naval intelligence. By the way he asked why you were still a Lieutenant? I told him your promotion to Captain was already in the pipeline."

Ian looked at both men smiling at him..

"So, the drinks are definitely on you, Captain Anderson."

Chapter 14

Sharon wondered how long it would be before, or even if, she would receive the call activating her mission in France. She knew some of the instructors had reservations about her ability to do whatever it took to survive. However, they all agreed that she should finish SOE agent training. Having recently finished training at Beaulieu she arrived back at her Auxiliary Unit and was assigned an operating area. As she approached the secret entry to her hidden bunker she instinctively knew something was wrong. Slowly making her way to the open entry hatch. Her heart thumped as she stepped over the edge onto the ladder's first rung. Silently she descended. When she reached the bottom of the ladder, she slipped past the first blast wall, and now she could hear the stranger's voice.

"Where are your code books," he hissed as he kicked Edward, the teenager who was the youngest member in Sharon's cell.

"We don't keep anything like that here. We are just a Home Guard observation post."

"No, you are not. You have automatic weapons and radio equipment. So where are your code books?"

Sharon crept closer, remaining behind the second blast wall. She spied the kettle and the coffee pot and hoped Edward's usual practice of keeping the coffee constantly on meant boiling water to throw at the intruder. Praying to herself and hoping the pain and shock would give her, and Edward a chance to overpower the intruder. Her hands were shaking as she prepared to spring into the room. Just in time, Sharon saw that the kettle was not on. Trying to control her breathing she frantically scanned the small kitchen area then spotted the open container of bleach they had been using to sterilise the area. Sharon knew she would only get one chance at a surprise attack. Taking a deep breath she burst into the small room, grabbed the can, and threw the bleach onto the startled intruder's face.

His scream filled the room like that of an impaled animal, yet somehow, he managed to grab Sharon around the throat and lift her off her feet.

What Sharon had not seen from behind the hidden wall was that Edward was tied to the chair and could not move to help her.

The intruder's fingers were choking her, and Sharon knew she had seconds before she passed out.

"Killing is not pretty. It's ugly, and you do whatever it takes to survive. You bite, you gouge, you shoot, you stab with all your might," Eric Sykes had screamed at the recruits in Arisaig. "And don't stop stabbing until you are sure they are dead."

Sharon frantically fought back, but he was too strong, and she felt her life slipping away. Her fingers found the scissors next to the map desk. Snatching them and, with what little strength she had left, stabbed the points into the stranger's left ear, the pressure on her neck immediately eased.

"Never give a wounded animal a chance to recover," Eric ordered. "Finish them off."

Sharon repeatedly thrust the scissors into the intruder's windpipe. Blood was everywhere as the assailant slid to the floor. Sharon knew no matter how long she lived she would never forget the look of horror on the dying man's face.

Later she had no recollection of freeing Edward or lying down on one of the bunker's cots. Edward switched on the radio and, with hands trembling, made the emergency call.

A young man in civilian clothes hurried over to the Brigadier.

"Sir, we have a breach in one of our special unit's bunkers."

"Where?"

"Between Canterbury and Dover."

"Is the site secure?"

"Yes, Sir."

"Make sure they keep the place shut down until we get there."

"Field Security Service are already on their way."

The whole area was cordoned off when Andrew and Ian arrived with the Brigadier.

"Who is the senior FSS here," asked the Brigadier.

"Sergeant Fyfe, Sir," Andy said, stepping forward.

"I'll assume everything has been contained."

"It has, Sir."

"I had better have a look," Andrew Hughes said.

"Who and where are our people?" Ian asked.

"An Edward Baxter and a Sharon Henderson. She is in shock and very shaken up." He pointed over to the van where she was sitting with a blanket draped over her shoulders.

Ian looked at Andrew and pointed to Sharon. Andrew nodded.

"You had better go and speak with her."

When Ian approached Sharon, she looked up a saw him. Her face was as white as a sheet. She started to stand up in the van, her arms hanging limply by her side, head bowed, then softly she started to sob.

Both Andrew and the Brigadier were shocked by the carnage they saw as they squeezed past the blast-proof wall into the now, blood-splattered small bunker.

The body was lying in a grotesque position, crumpled on the floor.

"That poor girl," was all Andrew could say.

"Is it okay to move the body, Sir?" asked a different field security NCO.

"Yes, that will be okay if the medical team are happy."

"We are," said the figure leaning against one of the bunks.

Andrew sought out Sergeant Fyfe and pulled him to the side. "You're the senior Field Security here?" he asked.

"Yes, Sir."

"What can you report so far?"

"I can only give you a detailed overview of Edward's incident report. As yet I have not carried out a formal interview with the young lady."

Two men approached the group, escorted by an FSS NCO. "Who is in charge here?" asked the taller of the two.

"I am. And who might you be?" replied Brigadier Gubbins.

"MI5. This is our investigation now."

"No, it's not," Gubbins said.

The MI5 officer smiled and said, "Yes, it is."

"Sergeant Fyfe here is in charge of the security of this military facility."

"What military facility?"

"This one. Now, we can work together as long as you follow Sergeant Fyfe's instructions. However, if you cannot comply, you can bugger off now."

Ian signalled for the FSS Sergeant and asked what arrangements they had made for Sharon and Edward and where they were to be taken for the incident debrief. Sergeant Fyfe told him he would take them back to London as soon as the site was secure.

"I will accompany you when you are ready to leave."

"It should be within the next hour."

Ian then went down into the bunker, and although the body had been removed, with all the blood splatters, the small field post looked more like a slaughterhouse than a field office.

"Does anyone know who the intruder was or anything about him?" Ian asked.

"From his wallet, it would appear he was a farm machinery rep and lived in Canterbury. That's being followed up on right now. We have a special unit hunting for enemy agents, many of whom, we believe, could have been operating here for several years. Have you heard of the German Brandenburgers?" asked the MI5 officer.

"We have," Andrew said. "Although I didn't think they would have been on the ground that long."

"We caught one last week who has been working here since 1936. And, of course, we have our own home-grown Nazis. Luckily, they are easier to detect because they can't help boasting to their fellow travellers."

"And I'm sure your people have that scene well monitored," the Brigadier said.

"We do."

The Senior MI5 officer insisted on being present at the debriefings in London. Andrew agreed on the provisor that any report would have to suppress the security operation being run by our Auxiliaries.

Ian travelled back to London with Sergeant Fyfe, Edward and Sharon, both of them clearly exhausted and had fallen asleep.

"Sergeant Fyfe. I am not sure, but have we met before?" Ian inquisitively asked.

"On two occasions."

"Really, I am usually good with faces."

"Both times were at Arisaig when I was participating with Free French troops assessing their security risk."

"Was that as part of the Field Police unit?"

"No, I joined just after the section changed from Field Police to Field Security Service. And because I speak French and German, I was attached to the SOE trainee section."

"So, we have met twice at Arisaig, and yet I didn't recognise you?" Ian said, shaking his head.

"Well, on both occasions, I was wearing camouflage face paint."

"Ah, well, I don't feel as bad then," he smiled.

In a secret location in the heart of London the FSS Sergeant along with Ian helped Sharon and Edward to two separate interview rooms. When questioned, neither Sharon nor Edward could add anything more to what had already been deduced. What later transpired from the debrief and further FSS investigations was the enemy agent had been seen wandering about local wooded areas. He may have been trying to discover Home Guard defence posts when he witnessed Edward approaching the bunker. As soon as Edward started to descend the ladder, he sprung from his concealment, ran over and kicked Edward in the head, sending him falling down the ladder before he had a chance to close the bunkers entry. It was assumed the stranger either didn't know how to close the entry door or deliberately left it open for a quick getaway. When Sharon approached the bunker and saw the entry open, she immediately knew something had happened and although she was initially going to call down to Edward to see if he was all right, she decided to silently climb down the ladder. Sharon's speed and initative stunned the intruder, but even in his agony, he managed to flail out and grab Sharon by the throat. Every training instinct for survival kicked in, and she was able to protect herself and kill the intruder. Her quick and decisive actions saved Edward's and her life. Both Edward and Sharon were commended for their actions in containing what could have been a disastrous situation, exposing Auxiliary units.

After the inquiry concluded, Edward asked to be dismissed from the Auxiliary, preferring to be part of the regular Home Guard. After ensuring he would not pose any security risk, his wishes were granted. After two weeks of convalescing, Sharon, on the other hand, had become more determined to serve with the Special Operations Executive and requested an overseas assignment.

Chapter 15

After the incident in Dover and over the next ten months, the threat of invasion was starting to subside. Ian continued to move between training with No 4 Commando and training British, French, Belgium, Polish and Norwegian SOE operatives. During that time, Ian got to know Sergeant Andy Fyfe very well, and both men discussed transferring to operational duties as opposed to training others for that role.

When Lord Lovat told Ian about his orders to work with and help train Canadian troops for an amphibious landing in France, both Ian and Sergeant Fyfe expressed their desire to be part of the operation.

"Operation Jubilee's mission is to establish and hold a beachhead at a port called Dieppe. It's being seen as a trial for a larger invasion to follow," Lovat said.

"What's the planned Commandos role?"

"We are to help train the Canadians on amphibious landings using the beaches around the Isle of Wight. As to the mission itself, the Germans have two main, heavy gun batteries one north and one south of Dieppe. Our mission is to take out the gun emplacements that protect the Dieppe coast, leaving the actual invasion to a mix of mainly Canadian troops, Marines and the Cameronian Highlanders. I don't think your Colonel will sanction you being part of this operation."

"Is it okay for me to look over the operational plans?"

"Absolutely, and if you can find a way to justify being involved, you know I am always happy to have you onboard."

Ian studied the plans. No.3 Commando was to approach from the north at Berneval-le-Grand and destroy the gun emplacement there. No.4 Commando would approach from the south Vasterival and neutralise that German Coastal Battery. The South Saskatchewan and Cameronian Highlanders were to take Pourville. The Royal Regiment of Canada would take Puys. And the 4th, 5th, 6th Canadian and 14th Calgary regiments, along with A Company of Royal Marines, were to take the port of Dieppe.

After studying the plan, Ian held strong reservations. His main concern was the lack of local intelligence. And the relatively low numbers of troops being committed to securing a beachhead. Added to his concerns was the use of inexperienced Canadian troops. Everything would hinge on three key elements. Firstly, the Commandos would need to silence the German's heavy artillery. The two flanking landings needed to be in place before the main force directly attacked Dieppe. And for any chance of success, the Germans must be taken by surprise.

Armed with the invasion plans, Ian arranged to meet with Andrew Hughes and the Brigadier. At the meeting, Ian went over the operations plan and voiced his concerns.

After hearing Ian's report, Brigadier Gubbins told the others what he had discovered.

"Stalin demands a western front landing to take some pressure off his Army. He is accusing us of letting him take the full force of Hitler's army while we stand back and do nothing. Off course, that's not true, but Supreme Command want to demonstrate their commitments."

"We are not ready for an invasion of France. Even if we successfully land troops and make a beachhead without immediate backup, we will be facing a Dunkirk-style evacuation."

The Brigadier looked at Ian and said, "Command has made its decision, the plan has been approved, and they will not change their minds."

"Then we must salvage something from the operation. I should land with..."

"I know what you want, and I don't agree to your proposition of involvement in, what I see as a straight-out Army operation," Andrew said.

"No 3 and No 4 Commando are part of the operation, and..."

"A limited part," interrupted Andrew.

"What's your proposal?" asked the Brigadier.

"I land with Lovat's troops at Pourville and take up an observation post allowing me to assess the effectiveness, or lack of effectiveness, during the main landing at Dieppe."

"What do you think of that proposal, Andrew?" the Brigadier asked.

Andrew Hughes knew Ian's proposal was sound, and if he was honest with himself, he would want to do the same. "It makes good sense."

Ian thought, in for a penny, in for a pound.

"I would like to request that Sergeant Fyfe, from FSS, be authorised to be part of the operation."

Andrew shook his head. "He is not an operational Agent. He's a security officer."

"Sergeant Fyfe would be an asset to this type of surveillance."

"He's Field Security not attached to No 4 Commando and has not undergone the Commando training."

"Andrew, he has assessed and accompanied more SOE recruits through their training than anyone I know, and he now wants to be involved in a new non-training role."

"Andrew, can we arrange a transfer for Sergeant Fyfe?" the Brigadier asked.

"We can."

"I will have to speak to the Operational Commanders and insist that Ian and Sergeant Fyfe be part of the Pourville landing group as special Intelligence officers." Looking at Ian. "You and Fyfe will be attached to the Canadians and will land wearing Canadian, not British Army uniforms, understood.?"

"Yes, Sir. Thank you."

"I will want a full report from you when you get back. And Ian, make sure you get back."

Chapter 16

Sharon sat silently in the back of the Lysander as she was being flown back to London for a special meeting with Colonel Hughes. The last eight months had been the most challenging time of her life. Her first covert mission was almost aborted just after she parachuted into southern France. At the drop were three members of the newly formed French Resistance. However, as she gathered her parachute, two of the group disappeared, leaving only their leader, Philip. And it was pretty clear from the first meeting that he did not approve of a young woman being sent to organise this region. Their first meeting was almost their last. Philip had demanded she must arrange for more weapons and explosives, then leave organising the resistance to him. Sharon stood her ground, although shaking inside and struggling to keep the pitch of her voice under control. She told Philip that her orders were to organise the resistance fighters into cells, anonymous from each other, and to start training key people as radio operators.

"That might be your orders, given from the comfort of some London office. But we are the ones here willing to fight the Bosh if given the weapons."

"I understand your position and your need to strike back. But we can't win the war with raw heroic passion. With your brave resistance fighters being caught or killed for no strategic gain. We must train our people, your people, to effectively share intelligence and be ready to rise when we are able to strike a decisive blow that will forever smash this occupation."

"Lovely words from someone who has not been humiliated and occupied, but we don't want platitudes. We just want guns. We are ready to fight now."

"That's not my orders. I have been ordered..."

"Forget your orders. Give us guns and explosives, or go home to your country cottage, and we will fight on without you."

Sharron could see the nods of approval from the other men who had returned and listened to the argument.

"I will help you set up district cells, and I will train your radio operators," noting he was about to interrupt. "Or I will leave and inform London that your people are unwilling to follow orders. And, as such, should be disregarded as a potential asset in our fight to defeat the Germans."

"Get your commanding officer on the radio, and I will speak directly with him," Philip sounded more in control, and his men stood about grinning.

Andrew Hughes waited by the radio. He had anticipated the reception Sharon might receive, so he was not surprised when the signal came in.

Sharon reported the situation before handing over to Philip.

"Colonel Hughes. We are ready to take this war to the Germans. But we are not prepared to have your person here dictate how we should organise and fight. So again, I simply say, give us the guns and leave the fighting to us."

Once more, Philips's men smiled and nodded approval of his strong stance.

"Will you please put the Captain back on?"

"Who?"

"The Captain."

Stunned, Philip passed the handset to Sharon. Andrew raised his voice slightly. He wanted the others to hear his instructions.

"Captain, I want you to ensure that every piece of equipment is ready for pick-up tomorrow night as per my contingency orders. This mission is over. Leave nothing. This sector will be removed from all future operational planning. And report to me when you get back. Over and out."

The signal went dead. Sharon started to repack the radio when Philip interceded.

"What does he mean we are removed from all future operational planning; we need to work together to beat the bosh?"

"Philip, I sincerely wish you and your men all the best. But my orders are perfectly clear, and if you are not prepared to follow orders, we are not prepared to support your endeavours." Sharon continued to gather her equipment into one pile.

"This is crazy, the Germans are walking all over everyone, and you want to organise small groups to radio London rather than killing Germans."

"We want to win the war, not bury brave martyrs."

Philip was stunned, he, and his men, knew he needed British support. He cleared his throat.

"I did not know you were a Captain."

Neither did Sharon. She had only recently been promoted from Auxiliary second Lieutenant to full Lieutenant to satisfy the hierarchy in Whitehall. Their protocol demanded all overseas agents hold the rank of full Lieutenant as a minimum. But she kept that information to herself.

"Can we start again and revisit your orders, Captain?"

"Yes, and please call me Sharon."

After spending months organising various resistance groups in France, Sharon had been called back to London. Her journey had taken weeks. As part of her brief, she had been told to help organise escape routes for downed pilots and escaped prisoners of war. Colonel Hughes had been working closely with officers from MI9. Ian Anderson had put together evasion training for aircrews. At Beaulieu, the trainers had coupled together various escape equipment, ranging from disguised silk maps to buttons that concealed a compass.

"Good morning, Sharon."

"Morning Sir."

"How was your flight?"

"Cold and uncomfortable."

"Wonderful," Andrew Hughes smiled as he showed her into his office.

"Would you like a coffee?"

"Yes, please, milk, no sugar."

Once seated Colonel Hughes went straight to why he had called her back to London. He briefly outlined the discussions he had been having with his special research and development scientists. His inventor teams from the Ministry of Defence and his secret workshops at Aston House, the Firs and Brackenbury Manor. The various facilities were nicknamed Churchill's Toyshops. All the independent groups asked him the same question. Did he think the Germans had similar weapons' research facilities?

Ever since he'd held these discussions, the question had been eating away at him until he decided there was only one way to find out. And that was to infiltrate the German Weapons Command Centre, GWCC

"And this is where you come in, Sharon."

"I am not sure how I come into this, Sir."

"When you were recruited, you said you had spent time studying in Berlin."

"I was there for over a year."

"And you speak flawless German."

"Yes, but I am neither a scientist nor an engineer."

"And that is exactly why I have arranged for you to spend time with Major Mills Jefferies and Stuart Macrae. They are the best in the field and have assembled a unique team of some of the most unlikely characters you have or will ever meet. Mills Jefferies, Stuart Macrae, and Cecil Clarke they will personally oversee your training, and when they are satisfied you have enough scientific knowledge, and only then, will you be put through an updated Beaulieu deep cover training program. You will also spend every day with our German training supervisor. She lived most of her life in Berlin. And finally, you will undergo evasion training overseen by Captain Anderson, whom you have already trained under."

"I have, and my mission is what exactly?"

"To be embedded into GWCC."

"As simple as that,"

"MI6 currently have some people working at a number of GWCC's facilities, but they are purely administration staff reporting on where the plants are, not trained field agents. However, 6 tell me they are confident they could arrange for you to be employed as a scientific administration secretary."

"When do I start my training, Sir?"

"Next week, so until then, relax and try to enjoy the next four days, then report to Aston House."

Chapter 17

Landing with No. 4 commando went smoothly. Ian was beginning to think they could establish a beachhead. Still, he genuinely doubted their ability to hold it for long unless they could completely support the troops on the ground from the sea and the air.

Having achieved their objective, No. 4 commando withdrew to return to their landing crafts. Leaving Ian and Sergeant Fyfe to observe the main landing at Dieppe.

What Ian did not know was that German naval ships had engaged with No. 3 commando while still at sea, and their planned assault was scattered, with only a small force of twenty commandos making it on shore. This force was too small to achieve their objective. However, notwithstanding their depleted numbers, they were able to impede, but not prevent, the northern coastal battery's ability to engage the main landing.

From their position, Ian witnessed the attempts being made by the Canadians, supported by Cameron Highlanders and Royal Marines, to try and clear the beach. But the German positions were able to rain deadly firepower on the troops. Added to their plight was the lack of armoured support. Many of the allotted tanks never reached the beach, and those that did either got bogged down in the sand, or, entangled in the lines of barbed wire.

It was evident that in less than six hours the landing had failed to secure a beachhead, and it was pointless to commit additional troops. The mission changed its objective, from an invasion to an evacuation. Ian witnessed countless heroic efforts to desperately retrieve as many troops as possible whilst coming under increasing bombardments from the coastal defences and the German Luftwaffe.

By 11 am, the fighting was over. The beach, now stained with deep crimson blood, revealed over three thousand men, either dead, wounded or taken prisoner.

Ian and Andy Fyfe knew it was hopeless to remain any longer. They would have to make their way inland, putting as much distance between themselves and Dieppe before German reinforcements arrived.

"How many do you think the jerries killed or captured?" Fyfe asked.

"I don't know, Andy, but we better move. Or we will be adding to the tally."

"I never thought we would be the first ones to try our evasion techniques," Andy said.

"Let's hope we got it right."

Back in London, Colonel Andrew Hughes was pacing up and down the communications radio room.

"What are we hearing from operations?" Hughes asked.

"Just raw data detailing how many we are bringing home and how many have been left behind."

"Do we have any idea of casualty numbers?"

"No, just numbers of the missing."

"Well, don't make me feel as though I'm pulling teeth. How many are missing?"

"Over three thousand troops killed, wounded or taken prisoner."

"Christ, over fifty per cent of the operation's landing forces."

"It gets worse, Sir. The RAF lost over one hundred aircraft. The Royal Navy lost a Destroyer and thirty landing crafts. And the Tank Regiment lost twelve tanks sunk at sea before reaching the beach. The remaining fifteen that landed were stuck on the shingle beaches or halted by thick wire and anti-tank obstacles."

"So all-in-all, a complete stuff up."

"We are yet to get a full debrief, but yes, I have to agree."

Hiding in dense scrub, Ian and Andy were checking out the railyard, trying to find a possible escape route.

"Ian, look at that engineer checking the engine's steam pipes."

"What about him?"

"That's Jean. I trained him at Arisaig."

"We need to speak to him."

It was dark and damp when the work's siren sounded the shift knockoff. Ian and Andy quickly made their way into the now deserted workshop, grabbed two pairs of overalls and workmen's caps. They quickly pulled the overalls on and then hurriedly made their way towards the group of men heading towards what looked like a beer garden. Most of the men sat there drinking wine. A few, Jean was one, were drinking beer. Andy waited until Jean went to get himself another beer when he accidentally bumped into him. For a fraction of a second, Jean scowled at Andy, and then recognition struck him like a blow to his chest. Neither man said anything, but Jean caught Andy's subtle gesture. Once outside, Andy told Jean to go back in, finish his beer, and then make an excuse to head back to the workshop.

Ten minutes later Jean arrived at the workshop, he walked to the back of the room and could just make out the shape of two figures standing there.

"Jean, this is Captain Anderson. I am not sure if you met him during your training?"

"I saw you once or twice," he said, looking at Ian.

"You've heard about the failed invasion at Dieppe?"

"Everyone is talking about it."

"We need to gather as much information about casualties and prisoners of war, and we need intelligence on how the German Command are viewing this assault."

"I have some comrades working in the hospital. They will most likely transfer the wounded prisoners from this station, so I can gather some of what you require, but not how the Germans view this."

"What about the bars where the troops hang out. Do you have any contacts there?"

"Yes, of course, I have a contact there."

"I am sure they will soon hear how it's being perceived. In the meantime, we need somewhere to hide, as the Germans will be searching for any troops that might have made it off the beach."

"I have a weapon stash hideout. It will be cramped, but it will be secure and dry."

"What about a radio?" asked Ian.

"There is one there as well."

"Can you take us there now?" Ian asked.

"You must stay here for another two hours until the bars are closed. Then I will come back for you."

When Jean returned for them the streets were deserted except for one bar. From the bar, Ian could hear the celebratory songs of drunk German soldiers. Silently the small group made it's way out of the town and through the woodland fields. At the hideout, it was agreed that they should have no contact for the next two days. Hopefully, by then, the Germans would have felt confident and dropped off their searches for escaped troops. Then, and only after that, would they try and make radio contact with the Colonel.

The following two days passed in almost silence. They could hear the cursing and swearing of German troops as they stumbled and fell, searching the hillside and the woods around the area. The rain was heavy for that time of the year, and the searchers were cold, tired, and sore.

They heard the whistle blast calling the search off for the day.

Later that night, Jean arrived with food and coffee, which both men devoured.

"I have some very sad news. Over one thousand of your troops were killed on the beach with many bodies still floating in the sea. There were also more than two thousand with varying degrees of injury, from minor cuts to double amputees. The most serious being sent to the major hospital in Rouen. The remainder of the wounded were loaded on trains to be sent to work camps in Germany. The remaining captured troops are being sent to Lamsdorf, five days by train to a place known as Stalag VIIIB. But for now, the search here has been called off, and the troops here have been praised by Hitler. Most of them have been given short leave and are again drunkenly celebrating back in town."

"Thank you, Jean. We must move soon, but first, I must contact Colonel Hughes."

The young Corporal knocked and then immediately opened Colonel Hughes's office door.

"Sir, we have had a short burst radio message. Attention: Colonel Hughes from IA and AF arrange pickup 02.45am S 17. NF K."

"Where is S17 NFK?"

"Envermeu close to Dieppe. I have checked, Sir, and we can't get them out tonight or even early hours tomorrow. They will have to hold on another day."

"Can we contact them?"

"We have arranged a reply time of 1.50am tomorrow morning."

"Good, make the arrangements."

Chapter 18

"Am I right to say that you have been to Aston House before?"

"Yes, Sir."

"Forget the ranks here. Everyone has an important role to play, rank does not come into it. Tell me, when were you last here?"

"Late 1940, Sir."

Millis Jeffries drew her a disapproving look.

"Sorry, Si," Sharon stopped mid-sentence.

"There have been changes since then, and after you have completed your time with my team I will hand you over to the Finishing School for further clandestine training. During your time here with my team, you will be introduced to various, shall we say, eccentric scientists, engineers, and inventors. But first, we shall meet with Stuart, who will gladly outline the scope of your crash course in our new weapons of destruction."

"Stuart, this is Sharon. She was here in mid-1940."

"Nice to meet you, Sharon. Can you run me through the hardware you were exposed to back then?"

"I have been here twice. The first time was as a member of the Auxiliary attached to the Home Guard."

"Ah, our Stay Behinders plan," replied Stuart.

"That's right. We were taught radio procedures and introduced to a range of weapons, including the Welrod silenced pistol, Sten gun, Tyre busters, and the Castrator. Then when I came back as an SOE agent, we were introduced to and trained in the use of C4 plastic explosives, Pencil detonators, Limpet and Lewis mines, and V-shaped charges. We were taught how to break into buildings, photograph documents, render vehicles and machinery unusable, etc."

"So, all your various sabotage training and equipment?"

"Yes, I suppose so."

"We have improved and added to your past training, but it is essentially the same. However, you were not exposed to our experimental Sections at the Firs and Brickendonbury. And while we don't intend to teach you how to make or use any of those weapons we want you to be able to identify similar projects that we suspect the German Weapons Command Centre are working on."

"I have to ask, why would you risk showing me your experimental weapons. Given that, I could be caught and forced to reveal what I've seen here?"

"Bravo, you are very smart, Sharon. You will be shown only what we have already developed and put into the field. But we will also guide you on what sort of weapons we suspect they are developing, including chemical weapons."

"Surely they are banned under the Geneva Convention?"

"Yes, their use is banned. But countries can still have them, supposedly as defensive weapons if attacked. However, we still need to be on the lookout, given Hitler's record to date," Stuart said.

"We also know they are producing and storing Heavy Water, necessary for manufacturing an Atom bomb. The Heavy Water is currently being processed at Vemork's Norsk Hydropower station. So, you see how critical it is for us to know their overall weapons strategy. And how close they are, or are getting, to developing chemical and atomic weapons," Jefferies added.

Sharon stared at the two men. "I don't have the scientific training needed for such a mission. I..."

"It's our teams' job to ensure we give you all the necessary training to enable you to recognise the type and scope of work being carried out. You do not have to understand all the scientific intricacies to identify where the particular projects are being carried out. That is why I want you to spend some time here with our scientists before you speak to the scientists at Porton Down's Chemical Weapons Research Centre. And

I can assure you by the time you leave your training here, you will be very capable of identifying Hitler's evil arsenal."

As Sharon spoke to Millis Jeffries, a car was waiting at Tangmere airfield as Ian and Andy Fyfe's plane touched down.

"Captain Anderson?" the young female driver asked.

"Yes."

"Sir, I have to take you to Colonel Hughes right away."

"We'd better not keep the Colonel waiting."

Less than an hour after touching down in the early hours of the morning, Ian and Andy Fyfe sat in a cold boardroom.

"You stay here Andy, while I try and get us coffee."

Ian found the deserted kitchen, put on the kettle, and searched for the tin of coffee he knew was there. Ian remembered the first time he had visited the then Major's office. He was pleasantly surprised to find they had real coffee, not Chicory. Hughes said the coffee was one of the few perks needed when you had people working long shifts with little sleep. The Colonel stepped into the kitchen just as Ian found the coffee tin.

"Black for me, no sugar."

With the three cups on a small tray, Ian returned to the boardroom where Colonel Hughes was talking with Andy Fyfe.

Colonel Hughes gave them an overview as far as he knew, of the scale of the losses, then staring at Ian, asked for an overview analysis of what worked and what hadn't.

"As you know I had misgivings about Operation Jubilee right from the first moment I heard about it. I believed the invasion force was far too small to succeed. But since the political decision had been made, it was a definite go-ahead. I knew I had to be part of the operation. So, as to what worked. Lovat's No 4 commando achieved their objective and withdrew without any casualties. I don't know what happened to

No 3 commando, but clearly, they could not silence the artillery battery north of Dieppe. All I know is that a number of commandos were taken prisoner."

"I'll tell you about No 3 in a moment, but please carry on with the main landing force report."

"I suppose we need to go back to the planning stage; a sustained bombardment of Dieppe was ruled out due to the proximity of the civilian population. Therefore, success depended on the element of surprise, completely silencing both heavy artillery batteries and getting off the beach quickly. Right from the start, it was obvious that the Jerries could still fire on the landing crafts before they even reached the beach. Furthermore, even though the RAF boys fought hard, the Luftwaffe had control of the air space. It could attack the support ships, sinking some and destroying landing crafts, many before they reached the beach. The troops and tanks that did make it ashore were met by a hail of machine gun fire. Almost all the tanks bogged down, and the few that got off the beach were entangled in the barbed wire anti-tank defence obstacles. And the rest, as they say, is history."

"I know you are still processing your thoughts, but what lessons can we salvage from Operation Jubilee?"

"As to the day of the landing, we would need a bombing campaign, that can significantly degrade the German coastal defences. We need to be able to direct effective shelling from destroyers close to the shore. The beach landing sectors must be thoroughly examined in the nights leading up to any raid.

On the morning of the landing, our advance party would then be in position to guide the landing crafts to the least mined areas. Just before the landing they would also need to create safe pathways for the tank landing crafts. Our tank commanders will have to develop a comprehensive plan to make sure they can get their tanks off the sandy beach."

"How will the advance party be able to carry out that role?"

"As I said, we would need the Royal Marine divers and engineers to map out the beach defences, especially those just below the water line. And devise a plan to avoid and/or blow up the mines before the main body hits the beach. We would also need all our SOE people in the area to organise the resistance on the ground behind enemy lines. They need to be in a position to carry out massive sabotage actions once the landing has commenced. The first twenty-four hours will be critical, and we need to hinder and slow down any German reinforcements arriving."

"Thank you, Ian, and Andy. I want you both to take a couple of days off and report back here to me."

"Sir, you said you would tell us what happened with No 3 commando,"

"Ah yes Andy, I did, sorry. As you know, they were to attack the artillery battery at Berneval. They unfortunately were intercepted at sea by a convoy of armed trawlers on escort duty.

The landing crafts were scattered, with only six landing at Yellow Beach 1. Clearly, they had lost the element of surprise, and all one hundred and thirty-five were killed or captured.

Only one landing craft from No 3 commando with twenty troops arrived at Yellow Beach 2, on the western side of the Berneval. These troops took up their firing position and managed to keep the battery silent for an hour and a half before running out of ammunition. Luckily, they managed to withdraw back to their landing craft and escape."

"Their valiant efforts will have saved countless lives that morning," Ian said.

"Of that I am sure. I have arranged accommodation, some cash, and a change of uniform for you both. Which has already been sent to your hotel room. My driver will take you there now."

Chapter 19

"It was a bloody disaster."

"It was a calculated risk that could have…"

"Could have nothing…"

"Gentleman, this is not helpful. Now, we have Captain Anderson and Sergeant Fyfe here who can give us their first-hand opinions and answer any questions."

The Brigadier looked at Ian and Andy before continuing.

"Captain Anderson and Sergeant Fyfe, thank you for your combined written report, which everyone here has had the opportunity to read. And I know there are several questions some officers have, but before I allow questions do either of you wish to add anything to your report?"

Ian looked at Andy and saw his slight shake of the head. "No, Sir, I believe we covered the main points, "Ian replied."

For the next hour, both Ian and Andy fielded numerous questions.

"I have one final question, Captain," the Brigadier asked. "Can you think of anything that could have changed the outcome of the day?"

"A miracle."

Colonel Hughes only just managed to prevent a smile.

One of the others piped up. "Are you saying there were no saving graces?"

Andy Fyfe spoke for the first time. "If I may?"

"Of course, Sergeant," The Brigadier answered

"In my opinion, there was."

"And what was that Sergeant?" asked one of the other officers.

"Someone had the sense to call off the landing before they were all killed or captured."

The room fell silent.

"Thank you, Sergeant. Colonel Hughes, can you, along with Captain Anderson and Sergeant Fyfe, meet me in my office at 1500 hours?"

"Yes, Sir."

"I shall see you then."

Colonel Hughes, along with Ian and Andy, left the room as conversations were just beginning.

Once outside the boardroom Andrew, quietly said. "We need to talk. Let's go and get a coffee."

"What's happening, Colonel?" asked a confused Ian.

"It's Andrew when it's just the three of us."

"Colonel. We had a deal," Ian said.

"Let's have that coffee."

Ian was still fuming inside when they entered the Brigadier's office.

"Come in, gentlemen. I'd like to introduce you to Professor David Campbell."

"Professor," Andrew said as he stretched out his hand.

"It's just David."

"David is a military historian at Cambridge University with a particular interest in Campaign Strategies."

"Like Carl von Clausewitz, On War?" Andrew Hughes asked.

"Yes, but I tend to focus more on Nicolo Machiavelli's Prince and of course, Sun Tzu's Art of War."

"So, in a nutshell, the ends justify the means, and all warfare is based on deception," Andy Fyfe said.

"Ah, Sergeant, I wish you were in my university class. Most of my students fail to grasp those key points. But from the Prince, I prefer 'Everyone sees what you appear to be, few experience what you really are.' And 'If an injury has to be done to a man, it should be so severe that his vengeance need not be feared.' But we are definitely on the same page."

"Don't let Andy Fyfe's Sergeant stripes fool you. It's a quirk of his military unit that they are all seen as non-commissioned officers," Colonel Hughes added.

"Sorry, Professor," cut in Ian. "I haven't read either of those books, but I get the gist. I am just wondering what myself and Sergeant Fyfe are doing here?"

"Let me answer that," said the Brigadier. "What you just witnessed was a dose of Inter Services rivalry. In that boardroom, there were conventional armed forces commanders, who do not see a role, or at least not a major role, for unconventional warfare. Then there are the Signals and Cipher operations who want to be left alone. Then there are our Weapons Research and Development boffins. Like the Cipher crew, they want to be left alone to develop innovative solutions to every imaginable problem. And that's before we get to the Spooks, both domestic and foreign. They are all very good at their jobs and are all strong-willed characters. I want them to put aside any egos and work collectively as part of a second front planning committee with two specific tasks. Firstly, to deceive the enemy as to the actual time and place of the invasion. And secondly, with the knowledge they obtain by assessing all the different services operations, they can prepare a detailed plan for the invasion of Europe. In that boardroom there were three planners we need to have working together. First Noel Wild, head of Ops B with years of experience in deception planning, most recently in North Africa. Next John Bevan, head of the London Controlling Section, skilfully works between the three different security services, MI5, MI6, and Special Branch. And finally, Montgomery's pick, Colonel David Strangways, head of R Force's deception staff. So, to answer your question, Ian. I need and require impute from Professor Cameron, you, and Sergeant Fyfe to be part of that process."

"Require?"

"That's correct. It's not a request."

"Can I speak freely, Brigadier?"

"Of course."

"When Colonel Hughes requested that I pull back from my Commando application, it was with the firm commitment that after we had trained our so-called Stay Behinders, I would be reassigned to a Commando Brigade. But, before that transpired, I was asked and convinced to remain with his unit until we trained recruits for the newly formed Special Operations Executive. I reluctantly agreed on the understanding I would then be assigned to a Commando Brigade, which, to be fair, has happened but on a kind of secondment basis. I joined up to physically fight the Nazis, not to sit behind a desk on a planning committee."

"Ian, I understand what you are saying, but our preparation for the invasion must take priority."

"My brother, cousins and friends are fighting and dying in North Africa, and I'm running around the hills of Scotland training others to risk their lives."

"I will guarantee you that once the invasion has commenced, you and Sergeant Fyfe, if he desires, can pick where you serve out the rest of the war."

"May I?" asked the Professor.

"Yes"

"Captain Anderson, I signed up for the RAF and started my flight training with fellow lecturers and undergraduates, only to be pulled out by the Brigadier. He convinced me we must win the war of misinformation, disinformation, and deception. So, I understand where you are coming from, but we have to put together a strategy that, as Napoleon said *Keep your enemy deaf, dumb, and blind*." Will you help me build that strategy?"

"I have no choice in the matter."

Banging hard on his desk and knocking over his glass, the Brigadier stood up straight and pointed to the door.'

"If you're not committed, you can leave right now."

Ian stood up, locked eyes with the Brigadier, and then turned to the Professor.

"You had better give me a copy of those two books to read if we are to build a joint strategy."

Ian turned and looked at Andy Fyfe, who simply nodded his acceptance.

Chapter 20

It was mid-morning on a bright sunny April day when Sharon, having just finished months of intensive training equivalent to a scientific undergraduate research student, found herself being summonsed to Whitehall. What now, she thought, more training. As she arrived at Colonel Hughes's office, she was told to go straight in.

"Philip, what are you doing here?" Sharon asked.

"I don't know. I was just told to come."

Colonel Hughes entered the office and looked at them standing by the map chart.

"You are probably wondering why I have asked you both here?"

"I am curious as to why I am here," Philip replied.

"I won't beat about the bush. Your regional sector is extremely important to our future plans, and that was why Sharon was specifically placed there. And of all the cell unit leaders, she believes you to be, by far, the most competent leader. Therefore, I want you to take over Sharon's regional coordinating role. That means you will have to appoint one of your people to fill your current role."

"And Sharon?"

"Sharon has been reassigned, so over the next week, she will brief you on your extended role. I have set aside an office for you to work from. Sharon will introduce you to your key contacts here in London and at Beaulieu. So, if there are no further questions? I will see you, Philip, before you return to France."

"And what about me, Sir?"

"We will talk after your handover to Philip."

The Colonel picked up his phone and called for his secretary to show them their office and the canteen.

Not far from Colonel Hughes's office, Ian, met up with David and Andy in their small, allotted office. He dumped his latest bundle of files on the large table in the middle of the sparcly furnished room.

"My head is spinning trying to sort out what this Section is doing and where its jurisdiction ends? And, I never realised for a minute, how many other sections Andrew and the Brigadier are operating. No wonder the Brigadier blew up at me. Why can't there just be one overreaching committee that can stop the numerous levels of duplication?" asked Andy.

"I think that's what the Brigadier and Colonel Hughes want us to investigate and make recommendations about. But first, we need to document the roles of each, shall we call them Silos, then look at how to best coordinate these secretive entities into a cohesive force. And then hopefully all sectors come together."

"I can't see any of the top brass handing over control to someone outside their section."

"I agree, their egos will oppose any other section chief overseeing their activities. So, we have to design a multi-tier reporting program that, on the surface, allows each section chief to remain in control, with some limitations. While at the same time eliminating petty rivalry and duplication."

"Easier said than done. Does anyone want a coffee from the canteen? "Asked Ian.

Both men nodded, and Ian left them, opening another box of War Office files.

At the canteen, Ian spotted Sharon sitting and talking to someone. Ian was sure he did not recognise the face, so he was not an SOE agent.

"Captain Anderson," Sharon's face lit up with a wide smile.

"It's just Ian here."

Her companion stood up and put out his hand.

"This is Philip. We work together in France, setting up resistance cells. Are you part of whatever Colonel Hughes has organised for me?" she asked.

"I don't know what the Colonel has planned for you, but I don't think it will have anything to do with what I've just been given."

"I suppose we will all find out soon enough," she smiled again.

"Yes, well, I'd better get back to my office with these."

"Whereabouts is your office?"

"The corner room on the third floor."

"Third floor? That's only three doors from our temporary office."

"Really? Well, I'm sure we will catch up again. I better take these coffees back before they get cold. It was nice catching up and meeting you, Philip. All the best with whatever the Colonel has planned."

Ian started to walk away, then placed the coffee on the table and turned back to Sharon.

"Are you staying in the city?"

"Yes, I am at the Thistle in Kensington."

"If you like, I could contact you, and we could try and catch up for dinner or a drink."

"That would be wonderful."

"Then it's a date or rather a drink. If I don't see you before you leave today I will call your hotel."

Ian was clearly in a more relaxed mood when he returned to their allotted office.

"Coffees and biscuits, "he said, smiling at both men.

Chapter 21

You could have cut the atmosphere with a knife in the War Office Cabinet Room when the Brigadier invited David Cameron to address the meeting. Assembled, were representatives from all the various military branches and executive officers of all the security services. None of them thought they needed to listen to a university academic and two SOE agents with updated reports.

"Thank you, Brigadier. Today I will be very brief. I know everyone here has a full agenda, and I am sure you hate wasting time in unproductive meetings. You probably just want to be left to get on with engaging and defeating Hitler."

Everyone in the room nodded, some even muttering about this, as an example, of a waste of their time.

"Well, gentleman, it's time to come to terms with the concept of a joint planning committee. You don't have to like it, but you have to work within it. And if you personally can't, then you had better nominate who will represent your Section at these meetings, because, believe me, your Service will form part of this committee."

"Who do you think you are?" said the head of MI6.

"Now you listen here, Professor," said the Admiral.

"Charles," the Brigadier said to the red-faced Admiral, who was already on his feet. "The Professor is simply telling you what Winston told both of us. I don't want to ask the PM to attend this meeting, but I will if I have to. Carry on, Professor Cameron."

"Everybody's voice will be heard on the committee and every suggestion examined, but once we, the committee, settle on a strategy, we all need to strive to see it succeed. Our job, in a nutshell, is to tie up as many German troops along their massive Atlantic Wall defences and to keep them under a heightened state of anxiety. By keeping the German High Command in a state of flux with them not knowing where and when the second front will take place.

We cannot let our individual pride and/or the views of our Services hinder or prevent a unified strategy to smash the Nazis. Gentlemen, I know for many of you, some of our plans will seem unconventional and outrageous, but we have to fight two wars simultaneously by preparing for the physical invasion and, at the same time, deceiving the German High Command. We will only get one chance of a successful sea invasion. We have to make it work. I am confident we can and will work well together to secure history's largest sea, land, and air invasion."

"Thank you, Professor. Gentlemen the PM has instructed me to finalise the committee members today, with representatives from each of the services, and agencies, with Professor Cameron being part of the inter-services planning committee."

The room fell silent.

"Professor Cameron will also have Captain Anderson and Sergeant Fyfe, who, as you recall, had witnessed first-hand, the desasterous problems encountered at Dieppe. They, by agreement, will meet with all branches of the services, highlighting problems encountered by the failed landing. Their role is to help establish a field advisory team, which will periodically report to the Campaign Committee. If there are no specific questions, I will adjourn the meeting until 1500 hours. Please ensure your committee's nominees are present."

The five men, Colonel Hughes, the Professor, Ian, and Andy, met with the Brigadier in his office.

"That went well," the Brigadier said.

"I am not so sure. I think most of the committee despise me," David said.

"Not at all, David. You are factually wrong. They all despise you, but they will comply. Now, what's your next step?"

"We will arrange to meet with each of the Services and ask them for a no-holds barred assessment of their current capabilities and their most pressing needs."

"You know they will all come to you with their Xmas shopping list?"

"And we will promise to give them as much as possible within the planning scope."

"Andrew, I know you have been overloaded but can you give us an overview of where you see the various parties' capabilities? Asked the Brigadier.

"I'll start by stating the obvious. Everyone is going to be demanding more resources. All military branches will demand more planes, ships, tanks, weapons, men, you name it. Then there is the Intelligence Services. They want more money for bribes etc. I need more SOE field agents and our own dedicated RAF crew and planes. And while we have been concentrating on France, we're still running major sabotage campaigns in Belgium, Greece, Italy and Yugoslavia. Plus, and we can't downplay this, our American cousins are making more and more demands. They want to run the show. In their view, he who pays the piper gets to call the tune. I think they will propose one of their people to oversee the committee."

"They already have, but Churchill laid out the processes we are currently applying. Ranging from, MI5's German Spy double cross program. Our boffins at MI(R)'s weapons research and development of dirty tricks, and our Commando training programs, which they are currently piggybacking on. Plus, our invaluable code breakers at Bletchley Park and our SOE and MI6 Agents in the field training and organising resistance groups. So, for the moment, they are happy to be an equal player, but they will barge in if they see any weakness of command."

Standing up, the Brigadier, for the first time, looked worried. His face was grey and drawn as he stared out of the window. Slowly he walked back to his desk and simply slumped in his chair.

"I have no problems with all our conventional armed forces preparing their people for various phases of the war. But we have one main mission, the invasion of Europe. Andrew, it's imperative that over and above running SOE agents in the field, you embrace MI5 and their Double Cross program. We need to intensify the frequency and quality of the intelligence we are feeding the Abwehr to ensure they believe their agents are being effective. I will ensure Bletchley has a team solely monitoring the German Intelligence communications. Our success, or otherwise, will be verified by their reactions to the information they are receiving. Ian, and Andy, your reputation as trainers precedes both of you. I know you are well respected by all the Commando Brigades and the Royal Marines, so I expect they will cooperate. Still, we also need to form a specialist engineering mine-clearing team, to work as part of our invasion landing special forces teams. And Professor, I need you to unleash your misleading and deceptive mind and work with our boffins to completely bamboozle the German Intelligence networks. We will only get one chance of pulling this off, so we have to make it work."

"With your permission, Brigadier, I don't think there is any value in either myself or Sergeant Fyfe attending any more of these meetings. We have formed enough contacts to immediately arrange briefings with senior Army and RM Commanders. Obviously, we will be in close contact with Professor Cameron. And will report on our assessments of each branch of the services."

"By all means, start building those bridges, but I want you both to be part of the invasion planning group. And Professor, I want a plan to be presented to the next meeting of the P.M, President Roosevelt and Stalin for them to give the plan green light."

Chapter 22

"How long are you back for?" Ian asked.

"I am not sure. I suppose it all depends on when my training instructors think I am ready," replied Sharon.

"And then?"

"At this point, I don't know. Can we talk about something else other than the war and..."

"Let's finish our drinks here and go for a walk."

After finishing her drink, Sharon stood up, pulled on her coat, and made for the door. As they started to walk through Hyde Park, she wrapped her arm through his. He smiled, and she blushed.

"Why the blush?"

"You're one of my commanding officers."

"Okay then, race me to that tree, and..."

"No, wait," Sharon said, and as Ian turned to look at her, she took off in a sprint.

"Why you..."

Sharon was smiling as he reached the tree. *Why is he looking at me that way?* she thought. Then Ian leaned into her and kissed her for what seemed a long time. Looking into each other's eyes, neither said anything. They simply embraced, then kissed again.

"Do you want to go for another drink?" asked Ian.

"No," Sharon replied, then pointed across the road. "That's my hotel."

"I didn't think we would get a car to use," Andy said.

"The Brigadier's got pull. And we have this with unlimited petrol, well within reason. What more can you ask?" replied Ian.

"First stop?" asked Andy.

"Portsmouth to meet with Royal Marine Brigade Commanders, then we head to Scotland. To Fort William., to meet up with Lord

Lovat, but we won't be driving that leg of the trip. It is over five hundred miles, so we will be travelling there by train."

"Sounds good. Are you planning to see your parents when we change trains?"

"I thought we might stop in Glasgow overnight on the way back, just in case Lovat has to leave early."

The two arrived at RM Headquarters, Stonehouse Barracks. And after a brief introduction headed straight to the operations planning room.

Ian and Andy again gave a comprehensive report on past strategies they had witnessed and additional strategies they would recommend as part of the second front invasion.

"So, if I am reading you right, we would have to send in recce troops for some time before the landing?"

"That's correct. We need to know the strengths and weaknesses of Hitler's Atlantic Wall. Our aircraft can see what's on the beaches, but we need to know what's below the high tide water line. Local intelligence says there are anti-tank structures and mines, but that's all we know at the moment. We also need you to take a Royal Engineer bomb disposal expert on each mission."

"Our troops can handle bomb identification; we don't need to have engineers tagging along."

"These engineers will be critical for clearing mine-free pathways off the beach. They will remove, mark, or explode them just before the troops hit the beach."

"This will have to be done in pitch blackness. Have you any idea how dangerous that kind of mission will be?" Asked one of the Marine officers.

"I have, and I hate to insist, but it will be critical to getting troops off the beach as quickly as possible. If they are pinned down, it will be like shooting fish in a barrel."

"What timeframe have we got to prepare for the landing, and where will it be?" asked a young Captain sitting in the back row behind his commanding officers.

"That has yet to be determined, but you can make a calculated guess at both."

"Well," the Captain said. "It can't be this year. We don't have enough time, men, or equipment, so we are looking at some time between April and July 44. And Calais or Dieppe would appear to be the obvious choice."

"I don't think it's helpful for anyone, and I mean anyone, to speculate on dates or landing targets. If we learned nothing from Dieppe, that would be a disaster. For our landing force to make and hold a beachhead we need surprise on our side. The Jerries know we will have to come at some point, and they will be waiting to repel our boys off the beach. So, it falls to you and your Marines to give them every chance to survive those first few hours."

"If we are to get a foothold on France, the beach landing area will have to be far longer than the beach was, at Dieppe, "the General sitting close to Ian piped in.

"At this point, General, all options are on the table, and it could be a simultaneous multiple-beach landing."

"We would need to start working with the bomb disposal people right away," said the young Captain.

"Yes, I agree. We will be arranging that very soon. I am sorry I can't give you any more details as nothing has been confirmed. Everything is still in the planning stage. The only thing I can say for sure is we will only get one chance of pulling off the second front."

"I think that went well, don't you, Ian?"

"Yes, and that young Captain was really on the ball."

"So, how was last night with Sharon?"

"With Sharon?"

"Yes, with Sharon?" Andy smiled.

"It was a very pleasant night. We had dinner and a few drinks."

"Is she going back into the field soon?"

"Yes, but she is not yet sure of where or when."

"You have to make the best of the time you can get together. You know I am happy to write up all the reports if that can give you both more time."

"Thanks, but she seems to be on a very intense training program."

"Well, the offer's there if I can help."

"I plan to see her tonight, but then we are off to Fort William in the morning."

After receiving every sector reports, Colonel Hughes met with Sharon's trainers and personally thanked everyone for their input.

Later that afternoon, he had arranged to meet with Sharon, and after preliminary niceties, he outlined her mission. By the intensity and content of her training, it had been clearly evident to Sharon her mission would be in Germany. Still, she had thought it would be near the border with France, not near Berlin.

Once the Colonel had given her the full briefing, he asked if she had any questions.

"Colonel, I would have thought this mission would have been conducted by MI6, not as an SOE operation."

"I agree, if it was solely an information-gathering mission MI6 should take ownership of it. But there is every possibility this will turn into a sabotage operation, and you are clearly the best female operative with the skills to carry out the mission and who has first-hand knowledge of Berlin."

"When will I be leaving, Sir?"

"Your cover and employment placement is being finalised. You must be ready to leave in about a week, two at the latest."

Ian was sitting at a corner table in the lounge of Prince Albert Bar and stood as Sharon entered. Right away, he saw a look of sadness on her face. It was clear, even from where he stood, she had been crying.

"Are you alright?"

"I just need a stiff drink," Sharon replied with a weak smile.

When she told Ian her news, he sat quietly. And she took his hand in hers.

"We knew it was going to happen sometime soon."

"Yes, and while you, a schoolteacher, are away risking your life, I am running around the country training others to fight while I stay at home. I joined up to fight the Nazis, not to sit safely at home."

"I know your training role nags at you, but you have to know the training you have designed and delivered has helped, and, will help save countless lives. Ian, Colonel Hughes really likes you and would not keep you here if he did not believe he needed you. So please don't beat yourself up. Be proud that the agents you train will inflict more damage on the Nazis than any brave individual soldier could ever do."

Sharon leaned forward and kissed him. She could hear the murmurs of disapproval from the two women sitting at the far end of the lounge. *Bugger them,* she thought and kissed him again.

Chapter 23

"Have you seen how many training areas there are?"

"Yes, I have Andy, but the Colonel wants us to become familiar with all of them. He said it will help tie everything together."

"So, we will be giving Lovat and his officers the same speel as we gave the Marines?"

"They will need a general overview to put them in the picture, but their role will be significantly different. They have to be our rapid response brigade to link our sea landing divisions with our advanced airborne troops. It will all depend on surprise, speed, and aggression."

"The commando's role has changed; it's become more of a light-armed infantry brigade. I remember when it was first envisaged, then it's role was to act like small raiding parties. Now I see it more like the regular army's special forces."

As they exited the train, Andy saw the jeep and driver.

"The Brigadier is on an exercise and will join you in a couple of hours. He asked if you could meet him later for drinks. He suggested Geaghan's Bar around seven tonight. Would you like me to drop you off at your hotel."

"We are fine. Our hotel is just across the square."

"When did Lord Lovat get promoted to Brigadier? The last I heard, he was a Major?" asked Andy.

"Recently, as far as I know, it was when he was appointed Commander of the newly formed 1st Special Services Brigade," replied Ian.

After checking in, Ian and Andy strolled into the town. Every local they passed on the street nodded and wished them a good day. It was clear they were used to seeing men in various uniforms.

They met again at six, ate dinner, then made their way to Geaghan's bar and waited for the Brigadier.

"Ian," Lovat called out as he breezed into the bar.

"Brigadier."

"Enough of that. Good to see you, and you, Andy."

"What would you like to drink?" asked Andy.

"A pint would go down a treat."

"Did your exercise go well?"

"Not so good, Ian. Our raiding parties boats were captured before we could get off the island. But it will help sharpen everyone's skills. So, tell me, since we haven't met since Dieppe, what happened after we pulled out."

"I assume you have read the report."

"I've read the official report, but you could drive a bus through their assumptions. I want to hear what really happened, and then we can discuss what you are here for."

The following day the Brigadier sent a car for them, and they made their way to his temporary headquarters.

"From what you report, Operation Jubilee was doomed from the start," said the Major, the oldest man in the room.

"That's correct."

"Well, I hope the brass in Whitehall have a better plan for the next time."

"That's why Captain Anderson and Sergeant Fife are part of the planning team, Reg, and we are extremely fortunate they are." The Brigadier pipped in.

"I can't tell you where or when the second front will take place because that's not been determined yet. But I can tell you we have to be far better prepared to strike fast and get the troops off the beaches. Otherwise, we could be looking at a rerun of Dunkirk."

At the mention of Dunkirk, the room fell silent.

After a further two hours of in-depth discussion, Ian and Andy were dropped off at the train station.

"You know you both would be welcome back if and when you are free from Andrew Hughes."

"Thank you, I, we appreciate that."

From Central station they jumped in a taxi.

"Queens Cross please."

Ian was exited to be arriving home.

"Mum, Dad, this is Andy Fyfe. I've spoken about him plenty of times."

"I feel as though I've known you for years, son," Ian's mum said.

"Well, Mother, get your coat on. I think we better take these boys for a pint."

"I don't need my coat if we are going next door?"

"Na, I want to take the boys to the Highlander for a change."

"Aye a will need ma hat, as well as my coat," she smiled.

"Just get a move on woman, or it will be closing down before we can get a pint," Ian's dad jibbed.

Chapter 24

"They what!" demanded Andrew.

"The War Office Committee wants me to pass on their thanks, to Professor Cameron and Captain Anderson for their input. But, they have determined that the planning team will, initially, be drawn solely from Ops B under the command of Lieutenant General Morgan. After General Morgan submits a skeleton plan, a newly enlarged team will draw up the final plan for Churchill and Roosevelt's approval, before showing the invasion plan to Stalin. The enlarged planning committee will be a joint US and British team. The code name is Operation Mespot. And your people will not be part of the planning team.," Brigadier Gubbins said.

"So, effectively, the most experienced trainers and the only ones with first-hand knowledge of the Dieppe disaster at the Atlantic Wall are being dismissed from the planning?"

"Andrew, we have been ordered to focus on our SOE operations and leave the second front planning and preparation to Whitehall's chosen committee."

"You know their only saving grace is they had the good sense to keep Noel Wild from Ops B and John Bevan from London Controlling Section on the committee."

"They also have Major General Hobart."

"I don't know him?"

"He heads up an experimental tank unit within the 79th Armoured Division, and he has requested a meeting with Captain Anderson and Sergeant Fyfe. Apparently he has been working on various, and some say outrageous, additions to Sherman and Churchill tanks."

"Is he the only one who wants to speak to us?"

"No, but the others are being more guarded than Hobart."

"Well, at least Ian and Andy will be happy to be dropped out of this operation. I am not sure about the Professor."

"They are not out altogether."

"If they are not part of the committee, then..."

"Churchill was persuaded, or at least lent on, to give the top brass their way, but he wants a clandestine review of Operation Mespot."

"So, the Professor is still part of my team?"

"Absolutely."

Arriving back in London, Ian Anderson and Andy Fyfe headed straight to Colonel Hughes's office, where they reported on their meetings with the Royal Marine officers, Brigadier Lovat, and his officers. Ian could not figure out the Colonel's apparent disinterest.

"Am I missing something, Andrew?" Ian asked.

"We, you, Andy, and the Professor, are off the planning committee."

"We are. Why?"

"The top brass have never liked our section, and they lobbied Churchill and others to have our services dispensed with."

"Fine, I didn't want to be involved anyway. Are we to be returned to Lovat's Brigade?"

"The short answer is no. The longer answer is Churchill still wants us involved, behind the scenes, as independent reviewers."

"If he wants us involved, why doesn't he simply demand our input."

"The brass have convinced the Americans that we are loose cannons and must be kept out of the planning for the second front. They, in turn, convinced Roosevelt and Eisenhower to intervene, and as such, we are officially out."

"But he still wants us secretly involved?"

"Yes, and he is not alone in that desire. Major General Hobart from the 79th Armoured Division wants to meet with you all and discuss possible tank modifications."

"The 79th Armoured Division, why I know nothing about tanks, do you, Andy?"

"Nothing."

"Professor?" Ian continued.

"He doesn't want to talk to you about the operations of tanks. He wants your input and suggestions, on some ideas he's been working on for getting his tanks on and off different types of beaches. So, I have arranged a meeting with him tomorrow at Bulford Camp on the Salisbury Plane."

"Then what are we meant to do, sit and wait until someone gives us the plan to look at?" asked Ian.

"Ian, I know you are angry, but we have to put our emotions aside and remember we have an obligation to make sure as many boys get off the landing beach as possible. That is our objective, nothing more and nothing less. Oh, and pick up the Professor. He is part of your team."

Chapter 25

At the Armoured Divisions base, the team were taken to meet Major General Hobart, who was in a large hanger- like shed, standing on top of a very unusual tank.

"Ah, gentlemen, welcome to the 79th experimental unit. Let me show you around."

None of the three had been to this depo before. They were surprised to see the unconventional additions to Churchill and Sherman tanks.

"When I read your report on Dieppe, I started working on our current amphibious tank. Until recently, these tanks had very limited amphibious operational value. They were designed for crossing rivers and not being dropped off into the sea. I wanted tanks that can travel independently from their landing crafts miles from the shore. My people have adapted Sherman tanks by fitting two propellers at the rear and a waterproof skirt which will keep the tank afloat in relatively rough waters. Would you like to see a trial run of our DD tanks?"

"Yes, we definitely would."

"Splendid, follow me to our mock-up lake and landing beach."

A tank landing barge was about 500 yards from the artificial beach. And, to simulate rough seas, two tugs were churning up the water causing sizable waves. At the signal from the officer on the beach, two tanks drove off the craft and dropped into the churning water. After the initial bobbin, the tank settled and started to make its way to the shore. Once on land, the propellors stopped, and the tank tracks took over. The engine transfer from propeller to standard drive mode was smooth, and the tank effortlessly cleared the beach.

"Obviously, battle conditions would be much more challenging. That is why we are conducting trials off the Isle of Wight and the Moray Firth in Scotland."

"How fast can they travel?" Andy asked.

"We reached about 7 miles per hour, when we trialled this design on Fritton Lake and at Osborne Bay on the Isle of Wight."

"How far out at sea can they be launched?" asked the Professor.

"Two to two and a half miles from shore. Obviously, we would rather get closer, leaving less time to be a target and sunk. Now let me show you some of our other trials."

They spent the rest of the day examining a number of other non-conventional adaptations before arranging to meet again the following morning.

That night after dinner, Ian, Andy, and Professor Cameron spent over two hours discussing the various pieces of equipment they had seen. The three had been impressed by the demonstrations and wondered what, if any, propositions they could add at tomorrow's meeting.

"Personally, I think Hobart has done a fantastic job, and his inventions should be adopted. I can't think of any other suggestions to offer, but let's all sleep on it. Maybe something will turn up," Ian said, then, finishing his drink stood up. "See you both in the morning."

The next morning at the base planning room, a young Tank Commander gave a detailed overview of the Duplex Drive or DD Tank. He then went on to describe the Bobbin Tank. Here, the tank is fitted in what could only be described as a huge thread bobbin with a reel of canvas roadway. The tank would roll out the temporary road as it drove onto the beach. Another Tank, a Churchill tank, was fitted with a short-range 25 lbs mortar to be used as bunker busters. Yet another, called Crocodile, with a 300-foot flame thrower. And, finally, the AVRE tank with a boom-like a mobile crane, ideal for laying girder bridges.

"I am interested to hear your comments," Major General Hobart asked.

"Have you tried using the AVREs to lift and move the German anti-tank hedgehog obstacles?" David asked.

"Yes, Professor, we have, but at the moment we have a purchase problem. As the tank lifts the obstacle it starts to sink in the sand and becomes immobile."

"Could you pull them out of the way?" Andy asked.

"Well, that depends on the density of the sand. If firm, we probably could use that strategy. It's slow work, particularly if the sand is soft. Our trials show it leaves the tank too exposed and vulnerable to enemy fire."

"What about a type of bulldozer design?"

"Yes, Captain Anderson, we are trialling that as we speak. So hopefully, we will be able to incorporate that into our landing suite of funnies."

"And, now for the main landing requirement, clearing anti-personnel mines."

"I was saving that for our demonstration after the meeting, but, since you have brought it up. We have designed what we are calling the Crab. Using a Sherman tank we've fitted a mine flail, a number of whirling chain flails that could smash a path through any anti-personnel minefields. But here is the critical question. Are they anti-personnel mines or anti-tank mines?"

"I have given that a lot of thought, and considering the length of the Atlantic Wall and the amount of equipment and explosives needed to cover such an area with anti-tank mines, I assume the mines will be anti-personnel mines."

"You know what they say about, assume. It makes an ass out of you and me."

"And, that is why we propose a plan to answer your two key questions. The density of the landing beaches and the types of mines on those beaches." Ian answered.

"Arial photos cannot determine that. How do you propose to answer those questions?"

"We have already met with some of the Royal Marines' Special Boat Squadron and Royal Engineer bomb disposal experts. They are currently commencing training to make pre-dawn inspections of all the proposed landing sites, once they have been confirmed."

"Now I can see why this team is still in the picture."

"On another matter," David said. "Has anyone considered our deception strategy?"

"Sorry, our what?" Hobart said.

"We need Hitler to believe we have at least double the tanks we actually have."

"And how do you propose we do that?"

"Inflatable dummies."

Chapter 26

"When were you last in Berlin?" Helga asked Sharon.

"Six years ago, and it was getting scary even then."

"The Gestapo have become even more paranoid, since then, so you will have to go and live in Berlin for at least a week to reorientate yourself before you take up the position at Spandau."

"Okay," Sharon said.

"But you have to understand, Berlin is being bombed most nights."

"I lived through the London Blitz," was all Sharon said.

Walking through the streets of Berlin in the daylight showed how much damage the RAF and US bombers were inflicting on the German capital. Even though no one would say it publicly, many Germans were beginning to fear the retributions that would be laid on them.

"Do you need more time to familiarise yourself with the city?" Helga asked.

"No. I am confident I remember enough to pass off as having been a student at Berlin University six years ago."

"Then Anna, Anna Moller, here are your papers, qualifications, and job references. You have to take things slowly, don't try to shine. Make friends, be easy going, and show a willingness to help anyone. We have a few contacts in the town who will help break the ice for you. Everything has been arranged for you to start working at Spandau Citadel in two weeks."

"What exactly do they do there?"

"That, Anna, is for you to find out."

David, Andy, and Ian arrived back in London exhausted from their two-day trip. As they approached their hotel, they saw him.

"Are you three up for a nightcap?" Colonel Hughes asked with a grin on his face.

"And if we are not?" Ian asked.

"Well, you're getting one anyway. And before you say the bars closed, I've arranged for us to have our own bar in the back staff room."

"Can we at least freshen up?" David asked.

"Take as long as you like, but no more than fifteen minutes."

Ian was the last to arrive twenty minutes later. He took a long pull at the already poured beer, then a sip of the single malt whisky.

"Major General Hobart wants you three to come and work with him. Of course, I told him you would never leave me. But he was very impressed. As were Lovat and the SBS boys. But now I want you three to take part in the next sensitive, no wait, very sensitive meeting."

"With whom?" David asked.

"Noel Wild, Major General Noel Wild, head of the planning committee."

"I thought we were on a secret mission. He's heading up the official planning committee."

"Hence the malt whisky. Look, Noel would rather you three were on his team, but he's been overridden, and he has been told that he is only the interim chair. He will be replaced by a US General once the plan has been approved. But he values your input and knowledge. It has to be on a need-to-know basis, but he wants to work with you three."

"Where do we meet?"

"Baker Street."

"Won't that be seen as a bit obvious we are working together?" Andy asked.

"That doesn't matter, as those that know what we do there, don't care. And those that don't know what we do there., don't matter."

"There will be hell to pay if they find out what we are up to."

"Let's make sure the brass are kept in the dark."

"And Churchill?"

"Who do you think arranged the meeting?"

"When do we meet?" David asked.

"Tomorrow, so one more drink on me, then to bed with you lot." Hughes smiled as he rang the bar bell.

Chapter 27

"I had rather hoped to meet your Churchill's irregulars at 121B Baker Street," Wild smilingly said.

"So, you're a Sherlock Holmes fan, Noel," Brigadier Gubbins asked.

"Can't get enough of his exploits. But we best get on with our business."

"If you are okay with this Noel, we don't worry about rank in this office?"

"Oh, that's fine by me."

For two hours, the group sat together in the small meeting room, throwing up basic invasion options. Everyone agreed that the invasion could not happen in 1943. There simply were not enough trained troops and, more importantly, insufficient numbers of essential landing crafts. Likewise, everyone agreed the invasion had to be between April and August 44. It was inconceivable that we could wait until 1945.

Further, they unanimously agreed that the invasion would need to be in France. And, from Bletchley Park's interceptions, Hitler and his generals had essentially come to the same conclusions. So, to successfully invade France, they had to somehow keep the German High Command blind to the date and place. Knowing that was the easy part, of achieving that, was their mission.

David walked to the blackboard. "Forgive me, gents, but I can't help the teacher in me." After drawing a rough outline of the French coastline, he added Norway, Italy, and Yugoslavia, although nothing was to scale.

"I am sure Hitler, and his staff, will never fall for a full-scale invasion Norway. Or even consider the main invasion could come through the Baltic region, with our troops linking up with the Soviets. But some of his inner circle hold real fears that a sizable, allied force, could smash through those regions and unite with the Red Army. And that fear alone will force them to commit tens of thousands of troops to defend those regions. So, along with the Soviet push from the east, we have to build the illusion of an invasion force launching from Scotland. Whilst, at the same time substantially lifting our activities in Italy, and the Baltic sectors."

"I agree one hundred per cent. But that still leaves us fortress Europe to invade," Wild said.

"So, Norway, Italy, and Baltic deception should form part of phase one. Now to phase two. I have studied your campaigns in North Africa. You effectively convinced the Germans that we had far more troops already in North Africa than we had in total. And that's what we have to do here."

"Please keep going, Professor, sorry David."

"We create two or maybe three phantom armies. One in Scotland, one in North Africa and the biggest in Kent, here in England. If we can have the German High Command forced to defend Norway and Yugoslavian, and at the same time, fool them as to our Channel invasion numbers, and, our invasion site. We can keep them strung out at a high level of anxiety for months on end."

"I concur with everything you have said, David. But what keeps me, and I am sure Hitler, awake at night is where will we land."

"How important is it that we take a port city, and if not the Pas de Calais, where?" asked Andrew Hughes.

'To successfully make a springboard for the invasion and to be able to supply transport, fuel, ammunition, and everything necessary to drive inland, we need to take and hold a port," Noel Wild said.

"So, it's Pas de Calais or Cherbourg, and from Portsmouth to Cherbourg is four times the distance from Dover to Calais. So, for a swift surprise invasion and to limit the armada exposure, Calais must be the favourite landing site," Gubbins said.

"Is a port absolutely critical to the first landing," Ian asked?

"Not to the initial landing. It is essential for the remainder of the landings and, more importantly, the ongoing resupply logistics."

"What about a temporary makeshift port until we can secure another? "Andy asked.

"What do you mean?" asked Wild.

"If we were to land at a beach or beaches that did not have a port facility, could we not erect one? I am no engineer but maybe someone could design a temporary floating port. One that could be towed over as soon as the first invasion force had cleared the beach and knocked out the immediate coastal batteries?"

"What a terrific idea. If the designers could build a temporary port, already fitted with rail lines, crane booms, and fuel pipelines, we could anchor it close to the shore., and quickly bridge the gap to the beach. I love it, Sergeant, sorry Andy. I will get people looking into that prospect. I am so excited by that idea because I am convinced the Germans believe we have to take a port town like Calais or Cherbourg. Now we can consider other options, such as the long stretch of beaches of Normandy." After noting the idea, Wild continued. "Colin, if you and Colonel Hughes agree, I would like to second Professor Cameron to my committee."

"I thought they wanted nothing to do with us," Andrew Hughes said.

"They did, but I rather think it was more to do with keeping SOE out, than the good Professor. In any event, I shall insist he is allowed to work with me, even if they oppose him being on the committee."

"Well, it's been a pleasure working with you David, even though it was only for a short period," Ian said.

"Likewise, but I still think we will, unofficially, be catching up from time to time."

"If you don't mind Andrew, I would like to tee up a meeting with yourself, Captain Anderson, and Sergeant Fyfe, with Major Jellico, the commanding officer of our newly formed Special Boats Squadron. He is very keen to increase small-scale raiding missions throughout the Adriatic. I think his plans and our strategy to have Commando raids regularly hitting Norway from Scotland and SBS forces, harassing German coastal defences up and down both shores of the Adriatic, suit our agenda."

"I am rather tied up on SOE operations, but Captain Anderson and Sergeant Fyfe are more than capable of representing our section and ongoing plans."

"Splendid, you will be hearing from me soon."

Chapter 28

Berlin was nothing like how she had last seen it. Sharon had felt sure she could navigate her way around the city, but now with half-demolished, bomb-damaged buildings, she could not be sure even of the area she had lived in. Luckily for Sharon, her cover story was that she had been living with family and friends in Munich for the last six years. Finally, she spotted one of the side entrances to Tiergarten. Sharon made her way to meet her contact as arranged at the park's main entrance facing the Brandenburg Gate. Both young women embraced as long-lost friends would, then made their way to the small garden café. The conversation was very light until they both felt it was safe to talk.

"Is everything arranged?" Sharon asked.

"Of course. Your work permit, past employer references, and accommodation details are in the basket."

'And the landlord?"

"They know nothing, and you need to ensure its kept that way."

"Can you take me there; I am having difficulties finding my way around?"

"Yes, but don't worry, many people have become disorientated by the number of roads blocked off. Partly for people's safety but also, for propaganda. Hitler does not want people to see the amount of inner-city destruction."

They made their way to the bus terminal to catch the bus to Spandau. Sharon felt very uncomfortable when she discovered her accommodation was less than 10 miles from Berlin. As soon as they arrived in the village of Spandau, Sharon saw the ancient walled Citadel.

"Is that where the scientists are working?" she asked.

"Of course, and they are expecting you to report for secretarial work tomorrow."

"What exactly do they know about my history?"

"You studied at Berlin University for two years before your family moved to Munich. You did not want to move, but your mother insisted that you do. Once in Munich, you met Fredrick and, after eight months, married. Shortly after April 1940, Fredrick joined the army. To all accounts, he was a brave soldier, and you were proud of him. Fredrick was so happy when you found out you were pregnant just before he was sent to Norway. You believed he was in a relatively safe posting, rather than the Eastern front. But that was not to be. A British-led commando raid attacked the fish oil factories his unit was protecting, and he was killed trying to prevent the factories' destruction. When you heard of his death, you fell into a deep depression. Refusing to see the doctor or eat anything. One night, you were found wandering the streets in shock. Your depression deepened when you were told you had lost your baby. For the last year, you have been slowly recovering, but you wanted to move back to Berlin and to be part of the might of Hitler's army that will crush the British forces."

"That's pretty full on. Am I supposed to be part of the Nazi Party?"

"No, but you can be outspoken about the progress Germany made once Hitler became Chancellor."

They stopped just around the corner from Sharon's accommodation.

"Your room is in No.5, the third house on the right. Remember Anna, you cannot contact me unless it's very urgent."

"I know."

"Take care."

Once settled in her room, Sharon remembered Colonel Hughes's final instructions. *This is a deep cover placement; you are there to gather critical information and identify a potential demolition plan. We will only contact you if we need to get you out. And you should only contact us in the event of an imminent threat.*

Sharon was confident her cover story would hold up to scrutiny. She knew she could do the scientific clerical role at the facility, but the most challenging part for her will be building and maintaining relationships with the research scientists and support staff. *I hope it's not too long before the Colonel is able to pull me out and let me get back to France.*

"When was the Castle built?" Sharon, now calling herself Anna, asked the senior office staff supervisor.

"They say the first fortress was built on this spot over seven hundred years ago. I don't know when the current Citadel was built, but I do know it was under siege during the Napoleonic wars, and I think that was when the heating last worked," she said with a pained smile.

Walking around the facility Sharon could recognise certain parts of the plant's process. Danger signs were everywhere. *This would not be a good place to be if the RAF boys attacked.*

"You will be working here in the administration wing and occasionally have to go to the laboratory. But the remainder of the Citadel is too dangerous, and you must not wander around the processing plant. Is that understood?"

Sharon nodded and said she understood.

"Then let me introduce you to everyone you will be working with. And then I will show you to your workstation where you can get started."

Chapter 29

"Are we ready to submit our plan for final approval?" Field Marshal Montgomery asked.

"Yes. We have to state the obvious. It can't be this year; we are simply not ready. And, for the invasion to succeed, we need surprise, backed up with shock and awe. The Port of Pas de Calais ticks most of the boxes. Shortest distance with a port for easy transport of weapons and materials to sustain the inland push. Our problem is that the German High Command would know that's our best option of getting troops into France. And, with that in mind, our planning committee unanimously recommends against Calais. Instead, we opt for the beaches of Normandy," replied Lieutenant General Morgan.

"How much longer would our troop ships be in the crossing?" asked Montgomery.

"Depending on the weather, roughly four times longer than if we were sailing to Calais."

"Have you estimated the size of the fleet, and how can we protect it for that amount of time at sea?"

"Perhaps it would be best, and maybe answer many of your questions, Field Marshal, if my team took you through a suggested scenario?"

"Please do."

For the next two hours, numerous charts and maps were brought out. The comprehensive report highlighted the requirement for the invasion to take place on a night with a full moon, essential for the airborne phase of the operation. This would limit the operation's window to early May or June next year. The flotilla would need both naval and air coverage as it crosses the 80-mile stretch of water. Our current estimates, and no doubt this figure will change, but we see the flotilla as having more than six thousand ships. This would be mainly made up of landing crafts, about four or five thousand, with six to ten battleships for shore bombardment. It was made clear to the committee that they, the planning committee, could not be more specific about numbers at this time but felt their estimate would be pretty close. The next group of advisers included Professor David Cameron and his team. He pointed out the need for a massive propaganda campaign utilising all the branches of our intelligence sections. He recommended closing off large sectors of land, both inland and coastal, to the general public. In these sectors, camouflaged equipment, both real and dummy decoys, would be held.

"For our deception to succeed, we need the Germans to hold their main Panzer Divisions in reserve. We need the German High Command to believe that Normandy is our latest feint attack and that our main assault is still to come in Calais. And for that to happen, the Germans need to believe we have more forces in reserve than we've already committed to Normandy," David said.

"How can we even try to convince them of that?" said the rear admiral sitting next to Montgomery.

"By creating phantom armies. One in Scotland and one in Kent. These phantom armies will have their own armoured support, hence the need for dummy planes, tanks, landing crafts, and established military camps. We will also need to ensure sufficient radio chatter, enough for the German subs offshore to pick up on. The phantom armies must also have high-ranking officers in charge."

"Have you anyone in mind?"

"I have not given much thought to the Army Commander in Scotland, but, if we want to make a really strong statement we appoint General George Patton, an officer, we know, the German High Command holds in high regard, to head the Phantom US Army Division in Kent." General Morgan said.

"Patton would go nuts and would never agree," said the most senior US officer, General Flood.

"He has to be convinced, and he has to be convincing. We would want him very visibly travelling to all his phantom units throughout the southwest," Professor Cameron said, then added, "and that means he will not take part in the actual Normandy invasion."

"I pity the poor bastard that will have to tell him that," General Flood said.

"You will, if the plan is approved," replied General Morgan.

Back at Portsmouth, Ian and Andy met with the SBS commander, Major Jellicoe. After discussing Jellicoe's plans for his squadron and his insistence that once his various raiding squads were formed, they work as a discreet unit.

"I won't beat about the bush," Jellicoe said. "I have spoken to Colonel Hughes, and he insists that both your secondments would have to enable you to be redeployed at short notice. And, as much as I admire what you chaps have achieved, it does not and cannot fit in with my SBS philosophy. I am more than happy for you to train with and give training to my men, but not to form part of our operational units."

"Thank you Major, for being up front with us. I will no doubt be speaking to Colonel Hughes when I get back to London. However, before I leave, I recollect you were part of our Dieppe debriefing some time ago. So you will be aware of my proposal that there would need to be advanced intelligence-gathering parties. Have you considered your people being involved in this phase of the operation?"

"No, my mission's brief is to harass both shores of the Adriatic, wherever possible, inflicting pain and terror on the Jerries. However, our sister section would undoubtedly be part of the main landing operation."

"Thank you again Major. I do hope we get a chance to work together."

"I am sure we will Captain, and, you too Sergeant."

Back in the car Andy Fyfe, clearly annoyed, slammed his door shut.

"What is the Colonel up to? Do you think the Brigadier knows about the restrictions the Colonel has put on our re-deployment?"

"Let's find out."

Chapter 30

"Colonel, can we have a word?" demanded a clearly annoyed Captain joined by what looked like an equally annoyed Sergeant.

"I assume you want to discuss what Major Jellicoe told you."

"Does the Brigadier know?"

"Yes."

"We had a deal," Ian spat out the words.

"And we have a war to win."

"We were available to participate in the planning group, but it was made clear they don't need, no, don't want us involved."

Colonel Hughes motioned for both men to sit down, picked up his phone and asked his secretary to bring them three cups of coffee.

"Andrew," Ian said. "Andy and I have done everything you wanted us to do, yet you are still blocking our re-deployment."

"There are major changes planned. You heard from Major Jellicoe about his operational role. And now the Commando units are being formed into brigades and will act more like vanguard, storm troops. However, the SAS still retain their hit-and-run role and is willing to be flexible in working alongside SOE. I can arrange your transfer to a SAS section today. You would be available to participate in any of their planned missions while technically working for SOE, effectively working between both agencies."

Andy spoke for the first time. "How exactly would that work?"

"If and when I need you, you work for me. And I need you on the ground between now and the invasion."

"To do what, sit on another committee or training program?"

"More and more of my time is consumed working with our, crazy but brilliant, engineers and professors planning our deception campaign. I have other valued field officers in charge of all our other regions, but I need you to be on the ground helping our SOE agents in Normandy keep control of the resistance fighters. We cannot allow them to fight indiscriminately. I have spoken to Philip, he's the local resistance leader who replaced Sharon, and he believes that he will be unable to keep the various groups in check. According to him, they respected Sharon, being an SOE Captain, and would follow her orders. But she's not there and can't be until just before the invasion."

"Why? Where is Sharon, and why can't she be there? This is our number one priority right now?" demanded Ian.

"She is on a sensitive mission that has taken months to prepare. That is why I can't pull her out until the last minute."

"We could go there now and sort things out."

"I need you both to assess our agents and their local resistance groups' readiness to spring into action at short notice without them thinking the invasion is imminent. We cannot afford them tipping our hand and starting to act prematurely. But I need to know their strengths and weakness. Also, I'm concerned that some of our SOE field agents may have become burnt out. Some of them have been there for years now without a break. I wouldn't blame them if they are getting desperate, but we can't fail now that we are close to the invasion. And that is why I need you guys more than ever."

When the meeting finished, Ian and Andy arranged to visit Beaulieu Estate for an intense briefing on all the SOE agents in the field. Here papers, and other supporting documents were forged, and an assortment of unconventional close-contact weapons were issued to agents, but only after they received comprehensive instructions on the use of these weapons and the could demonstrate competency. Finally, regionally appropriate clothing would be issued. The last point drove home the fact that they were moving away from a military operation, where if caught, they would be prisoners of war, to a saboteur mission which, if caught, would see them executed as spies.

"Do you think we will ever be free of the Colonel? asked Andy.

"No."

Four days later after leaving Beaulieu Estate, Ian and Andy arrived at RAF Tangmere airstrip, the home of No 161 Special Duties Service, attached to SOE operations. Andy stood by the hanger door as the pilot checked the four-engine Halifax, that had taken over the parachute drops from the older Whitley's, for the moonlight flight to France. Thirty minutes later, they were in the air.

At the drop zone, Philip, along with three others, took up a defensive position covering the only road usable by German patrol vehicles.

Philip heard the short radio burst and lit up his location beacon.

The pilot made a sharp coarse correction and then lined up the plane for the drop.

In the body of the plane, a red light lit just above the side door. Ian and Andy stood up and attached their static lines as the navigator opened the door. Both men looked at the navigator for his signal to jump. The green light came on, and he gave them the thumbs up.

Even though they expected the air to be cold, it still took them by surprise. But there was little time to ponder the cold as the distance between them and the ground rapidly disappeared.

Ian found the landing remarkably easy. While Andy, blown slightly off course, narrowly missed a huge rock causing him to make a last-minute jerk on his left harness, leading to an awkward landing. He was winded, but still trying to roll up his chute, as the resistance leader arrived.

"Are you okay?" he whispered.

"Just a bit winded, that's all."

Everyone helped gather the gear and then rapidly left the deserted field. After about an hour of uphill walking, three of the resistance group slipped away, heading to their homes. Leaving only Philip with Ian and Andy as they arrived at an old, rundown, farmhouse. The farmer met them as they approached the front door. He smiled a toothless smile and held up a bottle of brandy. Ian smiled back, and Andy simply nodded his approval.

The room was small, and sparsely furnished, only a solid wood table and four equally solid chairs stood in the middle of the room. After introducing his wife, the farmer put more wood on the fire and his wife poured everyone a drink.

"To victory," said the farmer. "Now we shall leave you to your business. Please help yourself to the rest of the bottle."

"What's the main problem Philip?" asked Ian.

"Politics," was his single word reply.

"You need to expand on that," Andy said.

Philip took a shallow sip of his brandy. "When we started our resistance we were an amature rabble, but in a relatively short time, with the help of training by SOE, we became more structured and purposeful. But as time went on, different agendas started to test and challenge our strategy. And now there exists the politics of the post-occupation leadership."

Andy asked, "How much pressure is being put on you and other group leaders?"

"I can't say for sure as I believe I am being kept out of the loop. The other leaders think I am too close to London. And I am sure you know that De Gaulle dislikes any British meddling in France's affairs."

"Colonel Hughes did tell me that he has had to split SOE's French section into two. The RF section provides support for De Gaullist groups, and F section deals with non-De Gaullist groups."

"I never knew that" Andy said.

"I just found that out myself before we left, but I had hoped it was a London-based problem, not one here in occupied France."

"I am afraid this has been going on for a long time, but no one wanted to risk losing the supply of weapons from London, so the division has been kept quiet. But now, as we head towards liberation, the cracks widen, and people are jockeying for command positions."

"Bloody great, just when we need everyone to come together, the rift opens" Andy said as he swallowed his drink and reached for the bottle.

Chapter 31

Sharon was shocked when she saw the extent of projects being developed at Spandau. She was familiar with the known nerve gas formulas, but she did not recognise this one. However, the attached notes sent shivers down her spine. These latest nerve agents were hundreds of times more deadly than Mustard gas and Sirin gas. *I need to get this to Colonel Hughes,* she thought. *If Hitler gives the go-ahead to use these weapons, the likely outcome of the war could change drastically. Would he risk Europe to win the war? Is he that mad?*

Sharon's brief was to find out what was happening at Spandau, how far advanced they were, and recommend possible options for neutralising the facility.

She set about writing several short single,-pointed, coded messages.

The scientists have developed two, as yet unnamed compounds, which are hundreds of times more potent than what's currently at Porton Downs.

The plant has underground storage tanks, which I believe could not be destroyed by bombers.

The processing plant, which I believe could be destroyed, but the timing would be everything. If the plant was attacked during one of the processing runs, hundreds of civilians could be poisoned and the land around the ground contaminated. Although I cannot say how bad or how long the contamination would last.

Irrespective of how we choose to deal with the facility, I recommend we draw up a plan to either capture the top scientist or eliminate him along with his assistant.

Sharon had to sit on the information until she could arrange a meeting with her Berlin contact. She was getting anxious, wanting to pass on this critical information to Colonel Hughes. Time passed slowly, then she was told to travel to Berlin and deliver a package to the Senior Scientist at Berlin University.

Sharon asked if she could have a day off to buy some personal items while in the city. "Of course, and while you are there, Anna, I would like you to pick up some items for me. I will give you a list. Now, remember, I only agree to one night. And if you decide to stay another night, you have to arrange your own accommodation," said the office manager.

"Thank you. One night will be fine."

Hughes read Sharon's messages and immediately requested a report from Porton Down's scientists on potential casualties if the chemicals were used as field artillery or bombs. He also wanted to know the possible contamination duration. Would it be hours, days, months, or years? His next call was to RAF Bomber Command, asking them to draw up a total or partial destruction of Spandau Citadel. But even as he made these requests, he was already considering either an SOE-only operation or, more likely, a joint SOE, SAS operation. And if that were to transpire, he knew the SAS troops he would demand.

The invasion plan had been drawn up and had Churchill's and Roosevelt's approval. Churchill was uncomfortable about not telling de Gaulle the allies' plan for the invasion of France. But Roosevelt was clear. We can't take the risk of supporting one French leadership over another.

"It does look like de Gaulle will get supreme control of French forces," Churchill said.

"Possibly, though not certain. And I don't trust De Gaulle to be straight with us. Let's wait and see how things develop before we say anything."

"The longer we wait, the angrier he will become. After all, we will be using Free French troops as part of our liberation plan for France."

"I don't care. I simply don't trust his agenda," was Roosevelt's final comment.

"Has anyone read the latest dispatch from Bletchley?" David Cameron asked his fellow committee members.

"Not yet. We were planning a debrief later this afternoon," replied John Bevan.

"You had all better stop what you are doing right now. Field Marshal Erwin Rommel has just been given the task of inspecting and bolstering the Atlantic Wall defences. And our source has heard he has a significant budget to increase bunker construction. He is redesigning the whole defence layout, from gun emplacements to beach minefields, concrete dragon teeth and their hedgehog anti-tank barriers. Apparently, he told Hitler they were not ready if they wanted to keep an invasion force stopped on the beaches."

"What's happening with Field Marshal von Rundstedt's 10th Panzer division?"

"We are not sure. Rundstedt wants to keep them nearer Pas de Calais for the defence of Paris. He is still convinced the main invasion will be at Calais. Rommel leans more toward Normandy. And Hitler sways from one to the other but has agreed with Rundstedt to hold the Panzer in reserve," Cameron said.

"Let's hope it stays that way. We really could do without Rommel being involved." General Morgan said. Voicing what everyone else was thinking.

Chapter 32

Neither Ian nor Andy realised how distrusted and disconnected the French resistance had become. Some of their best fighters were Spanish independence volunteers, exiled after Franco won the Civil War. These volunteers now in France hated Franco, who had been helped by Hitler. And for many of these volunteers, Stalin, was hated. During the Civil War Stalin had given personal orders making it clear that the socialists and anarchists fighting in the field were not to be supplied with Soviet weapons. He was happy to let the socialists and anarchists oppose the fascists with antiquated weapons while his well-armed Communist forces controlled Barcelona.

Then, there were the French communists, willing to take orders from Stalin to win a Communist, post-war France.

Opposed to them were de Gaulle's loyal supporters, who wanted to see the restoration of France's pre-war empire.

The news of Ian and Andy's arrival had been passed to each SOE agent, and arrangements were made for the agents to meet with them and Philip. Over the next two weeks they secretly met each agent in their respective sector on the night before they were introduced to the members of the resistance cells they controlled.

The plan was straightforward. Ian would meet with the cell leader while Andy would carry out an inventory of what weapons and explosives they had at their disposal. Then, the members, their leader, and the SOE agent identified the key targets earmarked for destruction. Most sectors had three or four strategic facilities to destroy. The main targets were railway bridges, communication aerials, and fuel dumps. Each team identified which members were responsible for each targeted facility.

However, as to who would order the attack, and when, was where the animosity manifested itself.

As far as London was concerned, the SOE agents and Philip would have the overall command.

Some of the groups accepted that order of battle. But others, bound by different associations, now pushed back.

"What does General de Gaulle say about you controlling Frenchmen?"

"I don't know. I am not concerned with the politics of senior Commanders. I have one job to do, and that's to ensure we have a coordinated resistance. Ready to spring into action at the critical time of the invasion," Ian said.

"And when is that?" asked one of the cell leaders.

"I don't know."

"Does General de Gaulle Know?"

"Again, I don't know."

"He should be the one to activate our actions."

"I will let the politicians argue that out. I have one objective, and that's to maximise the disruption to the German army's supply lines. If we are divided and fail to do that, we will be handing Hitler victory of mainland Europe," Ian replied while staring from cell leader to cell leader.

The room fell silent. No one looked directly back at Ian. As he stood up, and was about to leave the room., he stopped at the door, turned, and, in a soft voice, addressed all the leaders.

"If, by tomorrow, I don't hear otherwise," looking from one leader to the next. "I will assume and report that your cell is no longer reliable. I will recommend, and I am confident that it will be approved, that we cut off all future communications and draw up a new contingency plan. You then will be on your own, and if you act too early, you will be responsible for the failure of the invasion. And you will be responsible for the ongoing occupation of France." Ian spun around and marched out of the room, followed closely by Andy and the SOE agents.

Everyone in the room then started to speak at once. Philip held up his hand, and they all stopped talking.

"The Captain is leaving tomorrow, so we need to determine our position tonight."

Once back at the barn where Ian and Andy would spend the night. Andy poured Ian and the other agents a drink and then posed the question.

"How are we ever going to instil discipline and cohesion into those separate groups?"

"We've done what we can. It's now up to them."

Less than an hour later, Philip entered the barn. "All of the cells are committed to acting as one with one provisor."

"What's that?"

"The only person they trust from London is Sharon."

"I can't guarantee that Sharon will be here. I can guarantee to put their request forward. But I still need a definitive answer to my question."

Philip left the barn to pass on Ian's commitment to raising their request. However, he would also tell them that Ian still demanded an answer from them before he leaves tomorrow.

Back in London, Ian and Andy reported their findings to the Brigadier, the professor, and the Colonel.

"How bad is the rift between the resistance groups?" the Brigadier asked.

"Very bad. In fact, as it stands, I would have no confidence in the local cells working on a united front. But I am assured they will carry out their allotted tasks and will only act on our orders. What do you think, Andy?" Ian asked.

"I think they are capable and committed to their desire to fight. I think they could effectively slow down reinforcements that Rommel will be relying upon."

"It's critical that we halt these reinforcements for at least two weeks," David said.

"And our SOE team, how are they?"

"Tense, but still effective."

"How extensive is the flooding?" asked Andrew.

"It's quite extensive, mainly at the coast and then just inland from our designated Utah beach up as far as Omaha beach."

"Obviously, they must have considered the possibility of us landing reinforcements at the Port of Cherbourg. They know the flooded fields would create a bottleneck for our supply lines and make it easier for the Luftwaffe to strafe." David said, then continued. "That is why as well as sabotaging bridges, we are relying on our phantom First US Army, under Patten, to maintain the illusion that Normandy is just a diversionary assault. And Pas de Calais is where the main invasion will land. Smashing through to Paris."

"To get back to our original problem, how can we consolidate resistance actions?" asked the Brigadier.

"It's both Andy's and my opinion we can't solely leave it to the resistance to follow directions from London. We must send multiple small units to every critical sector and take command." Ian said.

"De Gaulle will be furious if we bypass his Free French forces, and the Yanks will also want to be involved." Colonel Hughes said.

"Then it needs to be a three-person team which must include a French operative. The teams can be configured any way we want as long as each team has at least one Frenchman." Suggested David.

"That would work. We have over a hundred French SOE agents in F section," replied Andrew.

"Andrew, I want you and the others to draw up a proposal for these units and where and when we would need to insert them. I will meet with the American OSS commanders and arrange a briefing."

The Brigadier stood up to leave. "I think we might just be able to pull this off. Even de Gaulle should be happy when he eventually finds out.

When the Brigadier left, Ian asked Andrew whether he thought the Americans would get on board with this suggestion.

"They will jump at the idea. But we need to start blending these teams right away."

"I am concerned there may be conflict as to the makeup and leadership of the groups."

"That is why I need you and Andy to be running the team selection, and more importantly their target allocations. So, it's back to Scotland for you two," Hughes said with a broad smile on his face.

"I told you we will never get away from the Colonel," Andy said.

Chapter 33

Ian, along with Andy and David, poured over the maps, highlighting the target areas and resistance personnel they had on the ground. And, in no time it became apparent that every SOE agent would need to be involved in the lead-up to the invasion in identifying strategic targets. And the estimated numbers they would need to deploy in order to secure success and, critically, the timing of when to act. Once that information was gathered, the special units would take control. Colonel Hughes had told them the unit's structure had been agreed upon, and the team training would start soon. For security reasons it was decided they could only be deployed in the field the night before the invasion commenced. That meant the SOE agents in the area had to start preparing the resistance groups even though they did not know the actual place or date of the invasion. All they were told was to make sure the groups under their sector would be ready to move at short notice. To give the agents some leverage, they had already started sending more weapons and sabotage equipment.

Philip contacted Colonel Hughes and told him things were really fractured. Even though the cells had committed to Captain Anderson, he still felt Sharon was the only person who could hold the group together. She had been there from the start and had won over their confidence. Under her guidance they had built a cohesive team. But now she was gone, and as much as Philp tried to keep the groups together, they still refused to recognise his authority to lead them. Andrew Hughes knew he had to make the hard decision. *Do I keep Sharon at Spandau, or as critical as that is, risk a fracture within the resistance just before D-Day?* He knew he had no real option; the invasion's success must come first, but maybe there was a way for her to leave Spandau for a month or two. He had to try. He would arrange for Sharon to be sent an urgent message telling her that her mum was critically ill. And her father desperately needed her home in Munich.

Hopefully, the Spandau Commanding Officer would agree for her to travel home to her family, making it possible for her to return there after playing her crucial role on D-Day. That way, she could still carry on with her mission. But, if there was no agreement by the Commanding Officer, he would have no choice but to pull her out, knowing she could never return. Andrew met with the Brigadier, who immediately concurred and told him to arrange for Sharon to be sent a message via the MI6 agent who had secured her position at Spandau.

All of the SOE and Commando training areas were now reassigned and had one job to do, blend together over one hundred three-man sabotage teams. These small three-man teams lived and trained together. Operation Jedburgh was born. Each team combination consisted of, a mix of; SOE agents and SAS troops from the UK, OSS officers and Ranger troops from the US Army, as well as a member from the Free French forces. Every team had to become familiar with their SOE contact already in position. As well as the region they would operate in, and, most importantly, the characteristics of the resistance team they would be leading.

As D-Day approached, everyone in the know was becoming very nervous. Whitehall was thrown into a panic in the months before D-Day when Leonard Dawe, the Daily Telegraph's crossword compiler and headmaster at Strand School, set clues and codewords for the newspaper, that led them to believe he may be a spy working for the Germans. In the months leading up to the invasion, his crossword puzzles included the words, Gold, Sword and Juno, the beaches assigned to the British and Canadian forces, these words were printed as earlier crossword solution answers. And during the month of May, his clues included the words Utah, Omaha, Overlord and Mulberry and were used in the Daily's puzzles.

This was not the first time this had happened. On August the 18th, 1942, a day before the landing at Dieppe, the word Dieppe appeared in the Daily Telegraph.

"What the hell is happening at the Telegraph?" demanded Brigadier Gubbins.

"According to MI5, who have investigated these breaches and interviewed the crossword designer, suspecting him of espionage, have concluded that, as in 42, the clues and solutions are a bizarre coincident," answered Colonel Hughes.

"I don't believe in coincidence Andrew. I want this school headmaster kept from supplying any more crosswords."

"That's already taken care of."

The phone in Hughes's office rang. Andrew picked up the receiver.

"Colonel Hughes'

"Andrew, I've just seen a report on the Telegraph's crossword. It's a disaster."

"Ian, I am with the Brigadier and, like you, we are deeply concerned. MI5 are saying it appears to be coincidental, but the paper has been directed to run any other planned crossword past MI5. Nothing has changed we are sticking strictly to the plan. Are your people all ready?"

"We are ready to go."

The brigadier took the phone from the Colonel. "Ian, I want to thank you and Andy for all you have done. I know it wasn't your chosen path, but both your contributions have given this historic invasion its best chance of success. Please pass on my thanks to Andy and know my thoughts are with you both."

"Thank you Sir I will."

In his operation room Ian was anxious as he sat, waiting for the signal to go. He knew, as well as every other planner of Operation Overlord there were only a few full moon nights in June, which was essential for the airborne landings.

Testily he stood looking at the phone, praying for it to ring. *Come on, bloody ring.*

The silence was shattered by the phone's bell.

"Get everyone to their respective airstrips. We are going in tonight. Oh, and one other thing I thought you might want to know. Sharon will be your contact at Caen."

"I thought she was on another mission."

"She was, but we had to bring her back. Philip said she was the only one able to coordinate all the resistance cells in the area. Ian, it's critical we take Caen, and the Americans take Cherbourg. I know I've said it before. We really need your teams to cut Caen off from the north while keeping access open to the beach. The plan is for airborne forces to take the canal bridge north of Ouistreham and hold it until relieved by Lovat's First Commando Brigade. And, if successful, they would only be 10 miles from Caen. It's critical we take the city or, at the very least, block the German reinforcements' route, to the beach. Sharon will be at your drop zone. And Ian, remember, I'm expecting that beer you owe me."

Ian gently placed the receiver on the cradle. And for a brief moment quietly reflected on the last four years. Everything and everyone they trained had this objective firmly fixed in their sights. And even though he knew the next few weeks would be critical, success in the next forty-eight hours was imperative. We have to get our forces off the beach and moving inland, if the invasions is to ultimately succeed.

All over the country, phones were ringing, and the airstrips were receiving the same orders. It was an immediate transformation from boredom to a hive of activity. Everyone was getting ready to board their plane when the order to stand down was given.

Some of the advance parties were already on their way when the decision was made to call off the assault and bring them back.

Disappointment reigned. The weather for the crossing was seen as too rough. So, the schedule was put back 24 hours. Emotions on the ground were mixed, with some feeling relieved while most were angry.

They had psyched themselves up, only to be left to go through the emotional rollercoaster again tomorrow.

24 hours after the aborted mission and just after midnight on the 5th, they were again ordered to board their allotted planes. The invasion was back on. Nervous smiles were everywhere. Ian heard someone saying, "Next stop France then Berlin."

Chapter 34

It was clear when they landed that the resistance members were keen to eventually take the fight to the Germans.

"Captain Anderson."

Ian turned and saw Sharon smiling at him.

"Captain, if I am not mistaken, you have already met Philip?" Sharon said.

"Yes, and we met again fairly recently." Both men shook hands.

Ian was surprised to see as many resistance fighters there to meet them.

"Why are there so many here?" he asked.

"We brought all our equipment with us so we could deploy each team from here rather than the farmhouse."

Ian called over the Jedburgh team leaders and, after quick introductions, attached a Jedburgh team to each of the resistance groups. The resistance cell leaders were angry and confused.

"Why are we being led by a British officer. We know our targets. We don't need to be led by anyone."

"The invasion is on, and our role here is critical. I don't have time to explain, but I expect everyone to follow orders or get the hell out of the way."

Noting there were no further objections, Ian started to deploy each group to their assigned areas. Two teams were sent to the railyard with their magnetic limpet mines to destroy as many engines as they could gain access to. Three other groups were to ensure that the bridges north of Caen were blown up, while another team was to protect the bridge just south of the city. One team was deployed with the task of bringing down the central phone communications tower. With Ian, Andy, and Sharon taking a group to sabotage the lead panzer column. Hopefully, clogging up the road and keeping the Panzer tanks immobilised within the city limit. The last team was to set up two heavy-duty machine guns, one at the main entrance to the barracks and the other opposite the officers' accommodation.

"Remember," Ian said. "We don't want any action to commence until we hear the naval bombardment, then execute your task and regroup at your new posts at the south bridge. Today is not a day to stand and fight to the bitter end for the city centre. We need to be mobile and keep the Jerries pinned down. At a minimum, we need to keep the Panzers tied down, preventing them from reinforcing Ouistreham. Capturing Caen is our ultimate objective, the very least we have to do is prevent German reinforcements from reaching our boys on the beach."

Silently the teams separated to position themselves for the imminent battle. Andy checked their equipment; plastic explosives with pencil detonators, graphite pastes for the tank tracks, with graphite compounds to contaminate the tank's fuel system. Not forgetting his favourite - PIAT Launcher, which he organised to be distributed amongst them. Slowly, they crept through the town until they came to the main panzer compound. Sharon and the three resistance fighters took up a defensive position leaving Ian and Andy the task of setting the explosives in place.

Ian and Andy had agreed that they should set their planned explosives in the officers' quarters before they started disabling the tanks. They had expected guards at the entrance, but luckily there were none. Their rubber sole boots made running through the building silent.

Ian expected that once it dawned on the tank commanders that they were under attack, they would head to wherever their command room had been set up. It was easy to identify the command room with its ceiling-to-floor maps of the Atlantic Wall defences. Expertly they proceeded to hide their explosives. There would be nothing left of this room when they went off. Next, it was out to the compound, where they saw three protected guard areas. Sharon had left one of the fighters to cover each guard post, and she moved to cover the door leading into what she assumed to be the tank crew's accommodation. The guards were aroused when they heard what sounded like small arms fire coming from Ouistreham.

"Do you hear that?" one of the guards asked.

It must be coming from anti-aircraft guns south of here. They have been bombing the area every night."

"I think it's much closer. Maybe we should wake the Colonel."

"You can if you want, but I don't want him taking his anger out on me."

"But..."

"What, do think it's the invasion," he sneered.

"No, but..."

"Go and check if you want. I am staying here where it's warm."

Andy was making good progress placing his explosives. He was able to lie underneath the tanks between the tracks, completely hidden from view, but Ian was having more difficulty trying to silently unscrew the tanks fuel caps without making any noise or being seen. In the end, he decided to give up on that plan. It was too risky and may draw attention to the explosives Andy had already placed.

Andy was just slipping out from under one of the tanks when the young German guard came from around the back of the tank. The guard was stunned to see Andy.

That moment of hesitation was to cost him his life. Before he could raise the alarm, Ian's knife had slit his throat. Ian motioned to Andy to help him drag the guard away. And although it was dangerous carrying the dead soldier out of the compound, they could not afford to leave him to be discovered by one of the other guards.

At first, Sharon was shocked when she saw Ian's blood-soaked sleeve before she realised it wasn't his blood.

"Why aren't they reacting to the noise coming from the canal area?" Andy asked.

"Probably because it starts getting noisy at this time every night," Sharon said.

"Hans, where are you," one of the guards called out.

"Leave him. He's a nervous fool," said another.

"No, I will go and find the idiot and get him to make us coffee."

Being so close, they heard the exchange and silently agreed they had to shut this incident down right away. Andy drew out his commando knife and silently slipped away from the group while Ian took out his recently acquired silenced pistol. Sharon lay in wait in case all hell broke out.

Ten minutes later, the group were back together.

"Let's hope there are no shift changes before dawn."

"I don't think that's likely," Ian said.

Even though all the teams in their respective locations expected the bombardment, it took everyone by surprise when it started.

Sirens started wailing, whistles blasting, and lights came on everywhere. The door to the south side main road bridge office was kicked open, and three grenades were thrown in. The explosion was almost deafening as the first two resistance fighters stepped into the room, firing their submachine guns. The long-term build-up of tension and excitement burst, and even though most inside the room had been killed by the shrapnel, it did not stop them from being shot as well. A whistle blasted, and troops started running south across the bridge to where the firing was taking place. When the troops at the front slowed down, suddenly realising they were being attacked, they regrouped then started to move more cautiously along both sides of the bridge. Almost halfway across, and with some of their confidence returning, the bridge violently erupted like a volcano, throwing men, machines, and masonry into the air before crashing into the river.

A similar scene was being played out less than two miles northwest of the road bridge, only this time on the rail network.

At the tank compound it was a series of one explosion after another. The crews came spilling out of their barracks only to be cut down in a hail of bullets. Those that made it back into the barracks came under fire from PIAT shells, fired directly through the door into the building, initiating a raging inferno within the old wooden building.

The expected mass spill out of officers from their quarters did not materialise. Those who did, only managed to take a few steps before being cut down.

"How long to go?" Andy asked Ian.

"Ten minutes."

The command room was still unoccupied. Then through the chink in the blackout curtains Andy had arranged, they saw the lights coming on.

On the coast road bridge south of the city wall, the guards were taking up a defensive position getting ready to repel any invading troops. Their heavy machine guns and two tanks were well-placed to slow or stop invaders coming up the road from the shore. What they had not anticipated was their attackers would approach from the north city side. And as such were easy prey, at least for the first phase of the assault on the bridge. Both their machine gun nests were destroyed in the first volley. The tanks fared little better, and the remaining few troops instantly surrendered.

"Do we shoot them?" one of the resistance fighters asked.

"No, we bloody don't. Tie them together, then tie them around the pillar next to the riverbank."

"Why?" asked one of the resistance fighters.

"Because they will have the incentive to tell us if the bridge is rigged with demolition explosives," came the reply from the smiling officer.

"Andy, fire a shell into one of the top windows. We need as many of them in the command room before it explodes. Sharon, you take the others back to the bridge."

Most of the teams had now made it to the bridge rendezvous and were looking for the best natural cover.

"How long do you think we will have to hold until we get relieved?" Philip asked Sharon.

"I don't know. If the airborne troops have captured the canal bridge and the other small bridges, the Commandos could be here in two hours. Assuming they are not held up by a German patrol."

"There were no patrols between the coast and Caen."

"Well, hopefully, they will be here soon."

At that, the last of the forward teams arrived back. They reported they were unable to get to the main tower as it was heavily guarded, but they cut phone lines and destroyed the power transformer feeding the radio room and surrounding buildings.

As they took up their defensive position, the officers' quarters blew up, sending flames shooting high into the air.

"Right, let go," Ian said as he lifted the PIAT launcher.

Andy started to move when a single shot rang out. Ian had moved about ten feet before he realised Andy was not behind him. Turning, he saw Andy's head down, slumped forward. Ian dropped the launcher and ran back to Andy. The bullet had struck him in the back two inches below his neck and had exited just left of his sternum in the chest. If he had not started to stand just before the shot, the round would have smashed into his skull. Ian dragged Andy further into cover and checked that he was still breathing. *That had to be a sniper shot, so where is he?* Ian scanned the building roofs and then the upper windows. Judging from where Andy had been sitting, it was down to two windows on the top left of the barracks. Having gone through his sniper training, Ian had a fair idea of his field of vision. *I need to drag Andy down that gully. It's our only chance.* He again checked Andy was breathing, noting that it was very shallow, and his pulse was getting weaker, but at least the bleeding had stopped. *That's got to be a good sign,* he thought. Before they moved, Ian retrieved his PIAT. *Where would you have positioned yourself if you were the sniper?* Taking aim, he fired a round into where he hoped the sniper was hiding.

Exhausted, Ian eventually made it back to the rendezvous point, where Sharon and Philip rushed to help him.

"Look after Andy. I've got to go back."

"Back for what?" Sharon asked.

"The PIAT, we are going to need that.

Chapter 35

At Germany's High Command Headquarters, a three-way communications link between the two field commanders and the Fuhrer was taking place. Field Marshal Rommel was pleading with Hitler to release all the Panzer Divisions and send them immediately to Normandy. But Field Marshal Rundstedt argued against that, saying this is a feigned attack, they want us to commit our forces, then they will launch the main assault at Calais.

"This is the main invasion," Rommel screamed down the line.

"Erwin, you are falling for Churchill's deception," Rundstedt softly replied.

"Enough," Hitler said. Then lowering his tone to a more thoughtful one. "Tell me, Karl," using Rundstedt's Christian name for the first time in months. "Why are you so sure Field Marshal Rommel is wrong?"

"Our, your intelligence, and the BBC English media show that General Patton, America's most aggressive Commander, is still in England. His ego would never allow him to miss leading the invasion. He plans to land in Pas de Calais and push straight on to Paris."

"And why, Erwin, are you sure Karl and all our intelligence are wrong?" Hitler softly asked.

"We have all read the Art of War and understand that all wars are won by deception. And, I accept the allies are trying to deceive us, but what is their deception? Is it this that's a feigned attack? Or is Patton, being in England, the deception?"

"I cannot find fault with either of your logic, but I am inclined to support Karl's opinion."

"Please, before you make your final decision," Rommel pleaded. "Please send half of the Panzer divisions. If I am wrong, we still have a substantial force to halt Patton. And at the same time drive this sizable invasion back in the sea."

"You make a good case, Erwin. Karl release two panzer divisions immediately."

"That's less than a third of the reserve."

"Erwin," Hitler's tone had again changed, now more aggressive. "Know when to accept a win."

Dropping the handset, the Fuhrer left his command centre.

Chapter 36

"You have to. I need you to take four resistance fighters, including Philip, and get Andy medical help. Hopefully, by the time you get there our boys will have taken the Canal Bridge, and you can give them an intelligence update. Then send Philip and the others back with more PIATs and ammunition."

"I can bring that back."

"Listen, Sharon, I want, no, I need you to stay with Andy. I want you there when he wakes up." *She had to be there for Andy. And he had to wake up.* Ian would not let, allow himself any doubt about that.

It was slow going carrying Andy on a field stretcher. As they reached the Caen to Ouistreham Benouville Bridge, they stopped to fully take in the fighting below them. There seemed to be a lot of glider wreckage in the fields and in the river. The airborne troops did not fully control the bridge, but they were making ground. Just further north of the bridge was an armoured patrol. From Sharon's position, she could see they were setting up a machine gun nest.

"Why aren't they firing on the bridge?" asked Philip.

'I don't think they can identify clear targets yet. But once our troops have taken full control of the bridge and are in the open, they will fire on them. Lay the Sergeant down here beside the tree. Then you two move up the slope until you are in a position to fire on those machine gunners. We will move in from the right. When I open fire, give them everything you've got."

The two groups split up. Sharon waited for the others to be in place before she would make her move. Satisfied they were in position, Sharon moved forward, watching the Germans' every move. The machine gunners were transfixed on the bridge, and she was almost level with them when one of them turned to pick up an ammunition box.

Without a second's hesitation, Sharon unleashed a hail of bullets on the unsuspecting gunners. Seconds later, after two grenades exploded, the machine gun nest was totally destroyed.

The attack caused total confusion to both sets of combatant troops near the bridge, with the airborne forces being first to seize the imitative and storm the last section of the bridge. The remaining German troops dropped their weapons and held up their hands in surrender.

Ten minutes later, Sharon, along with her four resistance fighters, and Andy, still unconscious on the stretcher, arrived to meet with Major Howard, the airborne commanding officer for this raid.

After a brief introduction and having handed Sergeant Fyfe over to the Airborne medical officer, Sharon brought Major Howard up to date with their exploits.

"I am afraid we cannot leave here. Our orders are to hold the bridge until relieved."

"I should be coming back with you, Philip."

"Sharon, you heard the Captain's orders. I know your history with them goes back over many years, so you know how important it is to Captain Anderson that you stay with Sergeant Fyfe."

"But..."

"Please stay with your friend."

With their extra ammunition, Philip and his crew started back along the road to Caen.

Firefighters were working frantically within the city to contain the two raging fires.

"What is the status of damage," the Caen German Commander demanded.

"Forty-eight panzer tank crew members killed, twenty seriously injured, fifty-three other ranks killed and one hundred and seven seriously injured."

"I don't want all the details. Just tell me how many tanks were destroyed. And how many officers were killed? I don't need all the other details."

"Sorry, Sir, sixteen tanks near the head of the column are undrivable. With seven more currently being repaired," then looking through his notes, the staff officer clearly rattled, coughed. "As far as I can tell, we have forty-three officers killed or seriously wounded."

"How the hell were there so many killed?" demanded the Commander.

"When the attack commenced, most officers headed to the Command Centre. And many there were killed when a number of bombs exploded."

"Bombs exploded inside the officer's quarters. Where were the guards? Get me those guards right now," screamed the Commander. "I want to know how they could have got in there and planted bombs."

"All the guards are dead, Sir."

"Lucky for them they are dead," the Commander said. "Do we have any prisoners?"

"No Sir, but one of our sentries is sure he shot and killed one of the Commandos."

"One of the Commandos. One. Is that supposed to make me feel better?"

No one answered what they hoped was a rhetorical question.

"What is happening at the shore?"

"It would appear the beaches are being overrun. The Bunker in Ouistreham is still secure, but they have lost contact with all the other posts."

"Get the tanks down there now."

"We need to clear the way out of the city and have sufficient infantry to move on Ouistreham."

"Just do it now."

Chapter 37

London's primary operations centre was chaotic.

Churchill, Eisenhower, and Patton were demanding up to the minute conformation of the landings. Reports were coming in every few minutes. Pieces on maps were constantly being moved.

"Stop," looking at the gathered Brigadiers, Air Marshalls, Four Star Generals, and Admirals, all looking stunned at the cigar-smoking Prime Minister. "I don't care who, but I want regular, concise briefings, in the War Office Boardroom every thirty minutes starting from now. Is that understood?"

"Understood." Was the sole reply.

Churchill, followed by the other leaders, headed to the boardroom.

"Who will join me in a whisky?" he asked.

"It's only nine am, Mr Prime Minister," Eisenhour said.

"Yes, but only here in London."

"I will," said General Patton.

"Splendid."

A small delegation entered the boardroom and started setting up maps and charts.

"Before we go into the detail," Churchill said. "Answer me one thing, are we getting off the beaches?"

"We have made progress at Juno. Sword, Gold, and Utah beaches. But things are going horribly wrong on Omaha beach."

"I will come back to the others," Patton said. "But first, tell me about Omaha Beach."

"Early reports are that the German resistance and defences are much stronger than we anticipated. The casualties on the beach are very high."

"Are we getting any of them off the beach?"

"Not as yet. The room fell silent."

Eisenhower spoke next and simply asked for a general overview but demanded a more detailed report for the next hour.

Philip and the others arrived back at Ian's position.

"How is Sergeant Fyfe."

"He has lost a lot of blood, but the doctor says no vital organs have been hit. There were no arterial damages, so he thinks the Sergeant will make a full recovery."

"Great news. I need you to share the ammo with everyone. I'll distribute the PIAT launchers and shells."

Ian gathered his small team leaders.

"When they start coming, they will be very aggressive, so make sure your team is ready. Stopping the tanks is the key to slowing them down until we get relief. But if it becomes apparent that we cannot hold the tanks back any longer, start making a controlled retreat. You have all been trained on how to do this kind of retreat. So, it's your job to impress on your team how to achieve that. We have already bought the landing force some time. We will buy them more, but I don't want martyrism here. We still have a long fight ahead of us. Tell all your men they had done really well today and that many young soldiers are managing to get off that beach safely because of their actions. Best of luck."

Ian had already decided that he had to block the road to such a degree that no tanks could pass. His only solution required him to destroy both tracks of the lead tanks. Because of the steep slope and rocky hillside, the tanks could only travel down the road in single file. If, as he hoped, the lead tanks could not be dragged off the road, the Germans would need to engage them with a frontal infantry attack. Having run down the road earlier, he already knew where he wanted to set his trap. The front tank's, right track, would be the easiest to hit. He was confident the shot could be taken from a well-covered area giving his troops the best chance of escaping back to our defended positions. The left side had little cover and once fired, would expose the PIAT two-man team. Usually, two troops were necessary for quick reloading of the PIAT, making the retreat back to the lines far more dangerous. Ian decided he alone would take four launchers, thus not having to reload between shots. Giving him vital seconds to make his escape.

He informed his advance team of his tactic, and every one of the five thought he needed a second with him. SAS Lieutenant O'Neil, who had insisted on being part of this team, volunteered to be his second.

"This is not up for debate, Lieutenant," Ian addressed the young SAS officer who was part of the Jedburgh team that had destroyed the railway bridge. "I want your crew to position themselves to take out the right track. But only fire your first round after I've fired my second to Philip and the other resistance member. You'll both take a covering position. Any questions? No, well, let's get moving."

Once in position, Ian did not have to wait long before he heard the clunking noise of the lead tanks heading towards him.

"Oh ScheiBen," the tank commander screamed as the tank suddenly lurched to the right. The internal alarm blared, smoke filled the cab, and the red warning light spun. The crew started panicking.

"Don't open the hatch," shouted the driver, but his instructions were ignored. The hatch was thrown open, and the first crew member started to climb out. He was shot dead as soon as his head appeared.

Bang, Ian's second shell smashed into the first tank. Then the first shell from the right smashed into the tank. Followed almost immediately by the second shell.

Ian rapidly fired off his two remaining PIAT shells into the second tank, noting that Lieutenant O'Neil had done the same.

The Panzer infantry were slowly recovering from the shock of the sudden attack. They fired widely, not identifying any specific targets.

Ian dropped the last of his PIAT launchers as soon as he had fired into the second tank and was bolting across the open stretch of land, racing for cover. He almost made it to the trees when the high-powered round hit him in his lower back. His legs immediately buckled, and he fell face-first to the ground.

"Cover me," screamed Philip as he rushed straight to Ian, lying prone on the ground.

Chapter 38

"Come in, Andy son. Lovely to see you."

"Lovely to see you, Mrs Anderson."

"It's just Peggy. Now sit yourself down, and I'll put the kettle on."

"How has Ian been since he arrived back home?"

"It's hard to say, he was very quiet for a while, keeping himself to himself, but he's really looking forward to catching up with you."

The door opened, and Ian shouted he was home, hung up his coat and entered the kitchen.

"Andy, it's you."

"It is that." Both men embraced.

"It's so good to see you. How have you been since...?" Ian left the sentence unfinished.

"I'm good. I've been posted to Brickendonbury at the moment. Some of those guys are really mad, but great company. And you, how have you been?"

"He has been pushing himself, far too much. You tell him Andy, this bloody war is nearly over, and he should be looking to his future."

"Did I tell you we heard from the Red Cross; Frank was taken prisoner somewhere in Italy. He is okay, and he managed to send Mum a letter."

"I was so happy to hear from him. I hope he is kept at the same POW camp until this is all finished. Ah, here's your da now."

Ian's dad convinced them to go to the local for a drink.

"It must seem to you that we are always going to the pub, but that's not the case. It's just we want to enjoy Ian and your company."

"That was great news hearing that Frank is okay."

"What a relief for me, but even more so for Peggy. Have you heard that Ian wants to go back to France?"

"Yes, that's why he asked me to come and visit him. He wanted to know my position."

"Look, I don't know exactly what you boys have been doing, but I know Ian, and I think I'm a good judge of you. You boys have done your bit. Both of you were wounded on D-Day, holding some critical position. No one can expect any more from either of you."

Andy could see the anxiety on Ian's dad's face. He knew Ian was not being dragged back, but he also knew how Ian felt. Andy couldn't explain it, but he felt the same. They had trained others to fight behind enemy lines while they slept in their own bed every night.

Later that night, Ian and Andy sat up talking. Andy told Ian that Sharon had stayed by his side until he was taken back to England on a hospital ship. He also filled in the gaps of what happened after Ian and his team had jammed up the Panzer column.

The Panzer support infantry started streaming down the hill towards the bridge, where that young SAS Lieutenant Ron O'Neil had set up a defensive line. He'd ordered the others to pick up and use the captured German weapons, almost doubling their ammunition supply. Still, he knew, as valiantly as his men were fighting, it was clear they could not hold back the sheer numbers of German troops. He was about to give the order for a tactical retreat, when out of nowhere, he heard the roar of the RAF Spitfire. The plane bore down on the advancing German infantry, inflicting massive casualties and forcing them to break off their assault. Buying the time needed for reinforcements to reach the bridge. But the German defence of Caen was very determined, and it took weeks before the city was finally taken and liberated.

On the 8th of June, de Gaulle demanded, and, was given, command of all the resistance fighters, and command over all the Jedburgh teams throughout occupied France.

"I've arranged for a meeting with the Brigadier and Andrew Hughes on Monday," Ian said. "That gives me two days with my family. I know my mum and dad want me to stay on convalescent leave, but I can't. I'm requesting to be sent back into occupied France to work with the Maquis resistance groups. That's why I asked you to come and see me. I wanted to know if you would want me to raise your name. I know we had demanded that before, but circumstances and times have changed."

"I'd like to attend Monday's meeting if that's okay with you."

"Absolutely."

Andrew Hughes had arranged for the meeting to be at Baker Street. Walking back into that board room was symbolic for the four men separated by rank but not by candour. With the pleasantries over, Andrew Hughes spoke first.

"As to your request to go back to France and re-join the Jedburgh team operation. Sorry but no. As to returning to active service, yes, that is clearly doable. Unfortunately, I can't say for how long that posting will last. Could you explain the position, Colin?" Andrew said, looking at the Brigadier.

"Ian, Andy, I think you both know the level of animosity felt towards SOE and SAS. All Branches of the Military and Intelligence services want us shut down now. They say we have run our race. The only thing that is keeping us going is Churchill. And, privately, he is losing support within his own base. I have held a private discussion with the PM and requested that he allow me to run a completely covert operation. He, the PM, fully understands how passionate we feel knowing we trained hundreds of young men and women, some military but mostly civilians, to put their lives on the line operating in enemy-occupied countries. And the fact we know many lost their lives, some in the most horrible circumstances. And accepts we have many still unaccounted for. So it was not too difficult for me to convince him to let me send in a trained team to, if possible, find those missing agents. But over and above that I also want to know where, when, and what happened to those SOE agents and SAS troopers. I also want to know the names of the German officers responsible for giving the orders and who carried out the executions. I want those bastards caught."

Andrew continued from where the Brigadier had stopped, telling Ian and Andy what he knew so far. Mainly that a special Gestapo unit under the directions of Nikolas Klaus Barbie, Chief of the Gestapo in France. Barbie's orders were to track down SOE agents and British Commandos, applying their so-called interrogation procedure, read as brutal torture. They publicly executed our people and any local resistance supporters. But after leaving the executed bodies on display for hours, they always took the bodies away, and buried them in secret, hiding the damming evidence.

Andrew told Ian and Andy that they would officially be on the ground as an SAS unit, tasked with finding missing agents. "You will not be referred to as investigators. There is already a War Crimes Investigation Team whose job will be to find sufficient evidence to secure convictions, but," he continued, "we all know there is a world of difference between knowing accurately, who is responsible and what can be proven."

"I will arrange for you both to be given intensive specialised investigation training techniques and some other specific, illegal skills. Thankfully not all of the intelligence sectors are against us."

"When do we start the training?" Andy asked.

"Tomorrow. Let's meet at Beaulieu at ten."

An area had been set aside for the training. Crossing, what had formally been the main dining room, Ian was surprised to see an old man sitting and staring out the window. To Ian, he looked like a retired University Don. Noticing both men entering the room, the older man turned, and, with surprising agility, strode over to meet them.

"Gentlemen," he said, stretching out his hand.

Even before preliminary introductions were made, Brigadier Gubbins and Andrew Hughes entered the room from a different door.

"Ah, there you are, Francis; long time no see, my friend."

"You're looking well, Colin, though still up to your eyes in, how should I put it, ungentlemanly conduct."

"Well, we can't all be saints, can we?"

"True." Looking at the other three, he continued.

"This meeting never took place. We, except Colin here, have never met, and we will only use first names. Oh, and I don't care if it's your real name or not. Are we all clear on that?" asked Francis.

Everyone nodded in agreement.

"Obviously, I am aware of your planned operation. I am not sure if you know the War Crimes Tribunal is involved in all official investigations, and there is no way your plan would be approved." Looking from one to the other. "So, we can disregard any help from that sector. They will have prioritised targets, and I hate to say this, but your people will be way down the list, that's if they make the list at all. And they will only conduct on-the-ground investigations once we have total control of the area."

"That's far too late for our needs," Andrew said.

"I understand. So, my question to you?" he said, gesturing with a slow hand sweep of the group. "What are your objectives?"

"Our first objective is finding our agents, hopefully alive. For the others missing, we want to know what happened to them. Were they killed in action, executed, tortured, or taken prisoner? Where and when it happened, and by whom," Colin replied.

"I understand. What I need to be clear on is whether, as part of your operation, you also want to prosecute offenders?"

"Definitely, if we can. But, under these circumstances, what are our chances of getting a legal conviction?" Andrew asked.

"I wish I could tell you it would be good if you had solid proof. But the international courts will focus on the most senior of Hitler's advisers. Then it will consider only other high-ranking officers or mass murderers, but that will be years down the track. And I stress that's only if you have solid primary evidence. Without that, it would be relatively low."

"Then what's the point of us even trying to gather evidence if it can't lead to a prosecution?" Ian asked.

"You're not gathering evidence for a prosecution, my boy; you're gathering it as your defence following any possible actions you may take."

Ian and Andy looked at each other and realised, for the first time, it may be them who end up being charged with a war crime. And now they understood why they needed to learn the importance of gathering strong, defendable evidence.

Francis told Ian and Andy how important primary evidence, such as written orders, letters, logbooks, and reports, preferably with date and signature recorded on them, were. Photographs showing the faces of those involved in the incident, the location and any recognised landmarks were also substantial evidence. Not so strong are witness's sworn statements unless they can be collaborated. Francis told them that a witness's memories of events can vary widely from witness to witness. He said when interviewing witnesses, try and invoke all their senses. Ask them what they heard when they saw the incident happening. Was there a distinguishable smell? Was it hot or cold? Was it light or dark? Try to involve all their senses and emotions. Often people recall hearing a sudden screech before seeing a crash. Sometimes they tasted the acrid smoke in the air before seeing the fire. It is your job to tease out the information and accurately record it. And on some occasions, you may be able to gather physical evidence, a pistol that ballistics can match or a knife with dried particles of blood that forensics could use.

After Francis finished running over the main interview skills, and again reminding them how important it was to secure any evidence they gathered, he wished them well and then left them with one of his people to continue their crash training course in lock picking, safe cracking and general breaking and entry techniques. Neither Ian nor Andy minded the fact that up until recently, their instructor had been serving a three-year prison sentence for breaking and entering several stately homes.

"Sir, It's Captain Andrews on the line."

"Put him through, please."

"How are things going at Beaulieu?"

"We have completed all our training and are ready to go."

"Splendid, but before you do, I'm sending you back up to Scotland for a refresher course."

"I don't think that's really necessary."

"In order for me to approve your mission, I have to attach you to part of the SAS existing teams operating behind German lines."

"But..."

"They insist, and I don't blame them."

"And then?"

"It's off to France."

"They do know me and Andy, won't be part of their small operational teams?"

"Yes, they do. But you will be part of a four-man team. Philip from the resistance in Normandy and Lieutenant Ron O'Neil. You also met him in Normandy, will make up your four-man team."

"Are they ready to go?"

"They will be by the time Sykes and Fairbairn are finished with you both."

"Shit."

Chapter 39

Even though both men had in the past completed the commando-designed training, time and recent injuries had taken their toll. And it appeared to Ian that all of the instructors must have thought this was some unannounced training assessment. And, as such, made sure that both candidates covered every single aspect of the training.

"I can hardly move after yesterday's assault course exercise."

"Don't say anything. Here they come," Andy said.

Neither Ian nor Andy knew the instructor who entered the dining mess. He walked over to the urn, poured himself a coffee, and then made his way over to them.

"And how are you both today?" asked the Sergeant.

"A bit stiff and sore, but apart from that, fine," Ian replied.

"A bit stiff and sore. But I'm sure a few days rest will help with that," the Sergeant said.

Seeing the smile on the instructor's face. Both Andy and Ian waited for the follow on. But he said nothing, and Ian was just beginning to relax when the Sergeant slowly placed his mug on the table and stood up.

"Fill up your water bottle, grab some food and be on the truck in two minutes. We are going for a wee hike."

Deflated, both men slowly stood up and started to make their way to gather some provisions.

"Get a fucking move on, you two. The longer you take, the further I'll take you. Understood."

Neither man replied. It would just have been a waste of breath.

Back in London, Colonel Hughes had arranged a final briefing before they would leave for France. Ian was surprised to see Lieutenant O'Neil and Philip at the meeting.

"How was Scotland?" Andrew asked, with a massive grin on his face.

"I think you know fine well how it was," replied Ian.

"Well, you both look very trim," Andrew still had the broad smile written all over his face. "To Business."

The briefing highlighted the fact that MI6 was unsure whether Chief of Gestapo Klaus Barbie was still in northern France or if he had already crossed over into Germany. It iwa their belief that he may be panicking and was desperately trying to put as much distance between himself and the allies advancing forces. From what we can gather he still has all his files and has been ordered to keep them. The rumour amongst the Gestapo was that Hitler had reserved some secret weapons that, if needed, would be used, or threatened with their use to halt the Allies before Berlin. Privately some of Hitler's High Command were trying to arrange a new amnesty. But no one wanted to put this to Hitler because they knew he thinks Germany can be defended, and he is confident the allies, particularly the Americans, will not want a protracted war.

"Do we know the basis of Hitler's beliefs?" Andy asked.

"His people have been working on a new breed of fighter jets, much faster than anything we have. Added to this are his long-distance missiles, far superior to the V2's. And we now know his scientists have developed more deadly chemical weapons, which Hitler has, at least until now, refused to use. But everyone is getting nervous."

"Surely there is no chance we would agree to an amnesty, is there? "asked Lieutenant O'Neil.

"Stalin and Churchill will definitely oppose. People also think it's unlikely that de Gaulle would agree, but some think he might. It would depend on the terms offered," Hughes said.

"What about Roosevelt?" asked Ian.

"The rumour, and it's only a rumour at this time, is that Roosevelt is too ill and is no longer calling the shots."

Andy stood by the window, apparently staring at the bird sitting on the windowsill. Slowly turning around, he stared directly at Andrew Hughes. "Colonel, could the Germans request or demand an amnesty from prosecution?"

"It's possible."

"If your assessment is accurate, and if they were to make that request. Everything would hinge on the US's position. Surely, they would not agree. Not after Omaha."

"Ian, the US Congress has always been split on being involved with what many of them see as a European war. And the losses on Omaha Beach have made their voices louder."

"Meaning what?" Ian asked.

"Meaning many would want to agree and start bringing the troops home without further loss."

"What about the Japanese war?"

"If Germany pushed for amnesty, so would Japan," replied Andrew Hughes.

During the exchange, Lieutenant O'Neil and Philip sat silently, turning their heads from one speaker to the next. The room fell silent. No one wanted to be the next to speak. All weighing up in their head the gravity of what Colonel Hughes had said and what that would mean if, and, it was a real possibility, an agreed amnesty was enacted. We would never know the fate of over a hundred lost agents.

"Then we have no time to lose. We must jump tomorrow night," Ian said.

Chapter 40

"Colonel, it's the Brigadier on the phone."

"Colin," Andrew Hughes said.

"I have just heard from Francis. Barbie has been positively identified in Stuttgart."

"When?"

"Yesterday."

"Colin, I will have to rush and contact the flight., and arrange a new drop zone. I need to see how close we can get them to the Rhine east of Strasbourg."

"That whole area is a hotbed of activity."

"I know, but we have contacts with the resistance there, so we will take their advice on the best place for them to be dropped, to get them as close to the Rhine as possible."

"They will have to travel through Germany, in civilian clothes and without German papers. And almost every able-bodied German has been called up to serve in the army."

"Except essential workers and farmers."

"For all we know, Barbie might be coming back to France."

"He won't leave Germany and go back there."

The Brigadier knew Andrew was right. "Can they all speak some German?"

"Apart from Philip, they all have a working knowledge."

"It's your call, Andrew, but don't let Philip jump."

As soon as the Brigadier hung up, Andrew was on to operations. "I need to know if we have any SAS units or resistance leaders operating north of Strasbourg close to Stuttgart?"

Minutes later, he was informed there was a cell in Haguenau.

"Make contact with them and tell them to get ready for a drop near the Rhine."

"When is the drop scheduled for Sir," asked the radio operator.

"Tonight."

"I don't know if that will give them enough time."

"It will have to. I want the drop as near the river as possible."

Andrew was informed by the SAS team they could have a group ready and suggested a drop zone one mile east of Roppenheim. Andrew arranged to be linked through flight control to the pilot. After a brief discussion, it was arranged for Andrew to speak to Ian on board the flight. Hearing everything said between this Colonel and his passenger, the pilot checked his map and fuel gauge, then piped in.

"Colonel, we will be at our maximum range and will only have one chance, so we will need a signal from the team on the ground, or your guys will have to jump blind. I have done a quick calculation. Roppenheim is about 60 miles from Stuttgart, cross country as the crow flies."

"Can we get any closer than Roppenheim?" Ian asked the pilot.

"That's closest I could get you, and it's pushing the flight to the limit."

"Do we know where he is staying there?"

"We believe he is staying at a Chateaux on the outskirts of Leonberg, twelve miles west of Stuttgart."

"That drops it to about 48 miles. We can do that in two days," Ian said.

"The place will be crawling with Jerries. It's going to take you much longer," Andrew said

"I'm confident we can cover that distance, and I don't think there will be many troops patrolling that area," replied Ian.

Andrew considered Ian's proposal. "Okay, but Philip can't jump."

"Why?"

"He doesn't speak or understand any German."

"I can hardly speak German."

"Don't remind me, I know."

"Do we have any contacts in Leonberg?"

"MI6 has, but I am not sure if you will be able to make contact with them. The Brigadier is working on that as we speak. I will make contact with the SAS team and they along with local resistance group in the area, will guide you to the jump zone. Hopefully, the Brigadier will have arranged a rendezvous with the MI6 agent."

"We will be in touch when we can," Ian said, then ended the radio signal.

The pilot told Ian they would need to be ready to jump in fifty minutes.

Ian went back, grabbed his crew together and told them of the change in plans. Philip could not believe he had been ordered to sit this mission out. Shaking his head, he moved away from the others.

"Philip the Colonel was only passing on orders. It's not a reflection on your skills, it's just, you don't speak any German, and they think it's too dangerous, especially if we get split up."

"It should be my choice. I would not put the mission at risk."

"I know."

When the rear door shut, the noise in the plane lessened as the flight Sergeant made his way up to the cockpit.

"I take it the three jumped clear," the pilot asked.

"You mean the four?"

"That Colonel is going to be pissed off when you tell him," smiled the pilot.

"I'll be telling him nothing. You're the officer, Sir,"

At the drop zone, three figures rushed to meet them, helping them gather their equipment, then led them to an old, beat-up rusted truck. As soon as they were in the back, the truck spluttered to life, and they were being driven along what appeared to be a disused logging track.

"Are there many Germans in the area?" Ian asked the resistance leader.

"Yes, but their morale is very low, and they don't like patrolling this area at night."

"That's handy for us. Has there been any contact from London?"

"No."

They all agreed they should make as much ground as possible before it got light. At the very least Ian wanted to be well clear of the Rhine before daylight. He was surprised it didn't take them long to get a safe place to cross the river. While the others were getting things ready, Ian managed to make contact with Colonel Hughes in London.

"I thought I made it clear that Philip was not to jump."

"You did, Andrew, but he was having none of that and insisted he had the right to be part of the mission, and in the circumstances, I agreed. But time is short. Have you managed to arrange a meeting place?"

"Yes, there is an old, deserted church building at the west of the graveyard in Leonberg. The agent will be there between 22.30 and 23.30 for three nights starting from tomorrow night. After that, you will be on your own."

"Thanks, Andrew."

"Best of luck."

The crossing of the river went better than expected. Although it was cold, it was nothing like as cold as they had endured in the Scottish lochs. Right after Andy had checked the map, and took the bearing, they were off. They had committed themselves to get as close to Leonberg before day break, then find somewhere to hold up until dark again.

"It might be a bit risky, but I think we will make better time sticking to the road than cross country," Andy said.

"I agree. Let's go," Ian said as he picked up his small backpack.

They made good progress between midnight and five am, but since then, they had to quickly scurry off the road four times, with the last almost being too late.

"That's it. We have to find somewhere safe to hold up" Andy said.

"How far do you reckon we have travelled," Philip asked.

"About 24, 25 miles," Ron said.

"If we want to get to Leonberg for tomorrow, I think we need to push on for about another hour," Ian said. "But let's spread out further. I'll take the lead, and Ron, you take the rear."

Ian kept a fast pace for the next hour and thought they would have covered about another seven miles. Then he called a halt, having been forced to take cover twice in the last ten minutes.

It was agreed that they would sleep in two-hour stints, with Ron and Philip having the first sleep.

"You know there is no way we can take this Gestapo bastard prisoner?" Andy said.

"I know."

Nothing more had to be said.

The site of the deserted church backlit by the moon made the hairs on Ian's neck stand up. Ron had crept through headstones covering the right of the church's broken front door, and Philip likewise had taken up position on the left.

Ian had allowed Andy enough time to cover the rear before he silently crouched forward to the door.

"Stop right there." Said a voice from the shadows.

"I am Captain Ian Anderson, SAS special unit."

"I bet you are. Don't move any closer. How many are with you?"

"Three, they are positioned outside. Is it okay to come inside?"

"No, let me tell you how this is going to play. I have had to work really hard to be accepted by this community, and now I've been put in this position. I will give you the information you need, but we will never meet again. Is that understood?"

"Understood."

"Barbie was seen in Leonberg yesterday, but he hasn't been seen today. That doesn't mean anything in itself, but I can't guarantee he is there."

"No guarantees needed."

"He has his own people who don't interact with the staff at the Chateaux. The staff there are ordinary working people. They're not Nazis."

"I am sure, in the future, there will be many ex-Nazis saying they were never supporters of Hitler."

"I have gotten to know these people, and I believe them."

"Well, I hope they don't get in our way."

"I know all you are thinking about is your mission. But I'm telling you, these are good people, so save your revenge for the others."

"Look, I'm not here to argue with you."

"No, you are just following orders, aren't you?"

"Get off your high horse. I am trying to find out what has happened to our missing agents and troopers. So, if that's just following orders, that's fine by me."

A silence fell between them. Ian turned around and saw Ron gesturing to know if he was okay. Ian signalled that everything was okay. The hidden MI6 agent motioned for Ian to come into the church. She gave him a drawing of the Chateaux's room layout and a set of keys.

"At the end of the Chateaux's driveway, there is a dirt road on the left. I will leave a vehicle there tomorrow night." After a short pause, she continued, "I apologise for my comments. They were out of order. I hope you find answers and that you are able to save some of your comrades."

"I hope so too."

Chapter 41

The phone rang in Andrew's office. "Yes," he snapped.

It was the Brigadier's secretary. She had been told to let him know that contact had been made and everything was on for tonight.

"Thank you." Slowly he replaced the receiver. *Best of luck, Ian. I wish I was there with you,* he thought. *I really do.*

The night was pitch black at three am as the four men silently made their way to the Chateaux. Having studied the drawing the MI6 agent had given Ian, his team had memorised the layout. Barbie and his people had taken over the whole of the first floor. The Chateaux servants were at the back on the second and third floors. At the rear of the ground floor housed the kitchens, cold rooms, pantry, and a large change room with three showers and equipment for riding groups and hunters. From that room, there was a door to the basement wine cellar and heating system.

The place was in darkness and not even a sentry on duty. As agreed, Ron and Philip made their way to check the two rear doors, one from the kitchen area and the other from the changing room. From there, they would make their way to the main stairwell. Ian and Andy were surprised to find the front door unlocked. When the others joined them, they carried out a quick check to make sure the ground floor was deserted. Then Ron made his way back to the servants' stairs and took up position in case any staff made their way downstairs before they had left. The remaining three climbed to the first floor. Philip dropped off in a position to cover the rooms being used by Barbie's guards. Quietly Andy opened the door leading to Barbie's room, and Ian silently rushed in.

"The bed was empty. Barbie was gone. The room still had the personal belongings of Barbie and three immaculate uniforms hung in the wardrobe.

Ian whispered to Andy to follow him as they crept along to Barbie's second-in-command's room. Again, it was empty. In frustration, Ian entered the last officer's room, and there he was, lying sleeping. The officer was woken with Ian's left hand clasped over his mouth and Ian's knife pressed hard against his throat. In German, Ian asked if he spoke English. The officer nodded. Making it clear if he shouted, it would be the last sound he ever made, Ian removed his hand.

"Where is Barbie?"

"He drove to Munich this morning and will not be returning for another two days."

"How many others are here?"

"None, I am the only one here. I volunteered to stay behind. To keep an eye on his belongings."

"Why has he gone to Munich? Who is he meeting?"

"He has gone for pleasure only."

"Then his files are still here?"

"Yes."

"Andy, you, and Philip check and make sure the other rooms are empty. Then check Barbie's belongings. And see what's there."

"Why are you still here and not with the others in Munich?"

'I chose to stay behind because I hate Barbie."

"I'm sure you do, and you're not a Nazi. Am I right?"

"I am not. I joined the army twelve years ago when I was only eighteen. My family were poor, and I could not find work."

"Yet you are working with Gestapo agents?"

"After your invasion, Barbie demanded an army escort. I did not volunteer for this posting; I was ordered. And from what I have heard of his actions. I hope he is captured, tried, and executed."

Andy re-entered the room, and informed Ian that besides the four staff, they had secured in the kitchen, the place is empty. Ian, pointing his pistol at the German officer, told him to get dressed and then take them to Barbie's files.

The filing cabinet was locked, but that only took Andy seconds to open it. Every drawer had been allocated to a geographical district with files depicting individual towns or villages in the area. Clearly, there was too much information for them to read. They would have to take the lot. They had to pull gear out of their packs to make enough room for the files. As they were shoving the files into their backpacks, the officer caught Ian's attention.

"What?"

"If I could help further, would you take me with you as a prisoner? I am fit and would not slow you down, and I could help carry two backpacks."

"What further information?"

"If I tell you, I will be hung as soon as he returns. That's if you have not already shot me."

"If the information you give me is legitimate, I promise you can come with us as a prisoner of war."

"I think I am a good judge of character. The files you have are important, but they only relate to local civilians and resistance leaders. The files covered under the Fuhrer's directive to execute all commandoes and saboteurs were not in that cabinet."

Ian spun around and pointed his pistol at the officer's head. "Where are they?" he shouted.

He pointed to a safe hidden behind the curtains. Andy rushed over and tried to lift the box. It did not budge.

"It's bolted to the wall," the officer said.

"I can see that. Andy, can you open it?"

"If we blow it open, we might destroy what's inside."

Ian ordered Ron to go and get the truck and bring it here. Leaving Andy guarding the German officer, he went to where the staff were being held. He spoke to the older man and, after a few minutes, returned to the room with a hammer and chisel.

"That won't open the safe," Andy said.

"I know."

Ian started smashing holes in the wall above and to the sides of the safe. Immediately Andy saw his plan, and from his small pack, he took out two blocks of plastic explosives.

The Chateaux's outer wall and room window disintegrated, sending the sturdy safe tumbling and narrowly missing the parked truck. The whole team ran outside to where the safe had landed upright as though it had been placed there.

"Right, lads, let's get it onto the truck."

"You know when he discovers these files are gone, he will disappear, and we will never get him?" Andy said.

"I have thought about that. I am going to lie and wait for Barbie to return." Picking up his scoped rifle.

"I won't miss him, then I will disappear into the hills. I'm confident I can evade them and make my way back over the Rhine and on to Strasbourg."

"That's all good and well, but if we get caught in the process, because with you out, our chances of getting the safe back are reduced, and if that happened, no one will ever know where our murdered agents and troops are buried."

"Captain, can I make a suggestion?" the prisoner said.

"Sure, what's your suggestion."

"You don't use the truck."

"What then?"

"In the stables, there is a staff car and motorbike and sidecar."

Ian nodded to Ron, who ran over and pulled open the double doors. And, as the German officer had stated, there was a staff car, motorbike, and sidecar.

"My suggestion is that you will have a better chance getting back to the Rhine with the car than the truck. But I have a big question. Do you have commandos in the area?"

Ian did not answer right away. As far as he knew, there were no SAS units operating on this side of the river. *It's not a bad idea,* he thought, *but what if we get stopped. How do we respond?*

"Assuming there is not, we would still have to get past German patrols."

"If I sat in the front with a driver and you in the back wearing one of Barbie's uniforms, I believe we could get past any patrols."

Ian knew it was risky, but no more so than with the truck. He asked Ron to check both vehicles. Before deciding it was their best option.

"Are there other uniforms here?"

"I am not sure, but I don't think the guards would have taken all their gear away with them for three days."

After searching through the equipment, they managed to put together enough clothing to pass a cursory glance. Two coats and helmets for Philip and Andy, who would be on the motorbike, a private's tunic and cap for Ron, the staff car driver and, a tight-fitting officer's tunic and peak cap for Ian.

"You know if we get caught wearing these uniforms, we will be shot on the spot as spies," Andy said.

"If we get caught, we will be shot no matter what we are wearing," replied Ian.

With the fuel topped up and the safe placed in the trunk, they set off. Due to the fact that they could not risk putting on headlights and the road conditions, chopped up by numerous tank tracks, they had to drive slowly.

"This is torture," Ron said.

Then up ahead, he saw a roadblock, and the guard was waving a torch, signalling them to slow down. Instinctively Ian cocked his pistol and submachine gun, hidden under a blanket. Philip readied his German-made submachine gun in the sidecar, and Andy was confident he could fire his, which was strapped across his chest.

The car slowed and then stopped as the guard approached with his weapon pointed at the driver.

"Where are you going?" he demanded.

"We have prisoners to interrogate in Karlsruhe."

"My orders are to close off this section of road and let no vehicles through without specific documentation. You will have to wait until I can get authorisation."

"Do you recognise insignia?"

"Of course."

"So, you, no one else, will take the responsibility of impeding a Gestapo interrogation. You are either very brave or foolish. No, that's not right. You are just stupid."

At the mention of him being responsible for delaying Gestapo officers, the guard seemed to shrink before their eyes.

"Open the road," he shouted to the other guards, who immediately drove their vehicle blocking the road to the verge. The guard then saluted as Ron slipped the car into gear and drove off, with Andy following close behind.

"Do you think he will radio ahead?" Ron asked.

"I am not sure, but we will soon find out," Ian answered.

Chapter 42

Colonel Hughes had just fallen asleep on the old couch when Corporal Williams entered his office and woke him. Sleepily, Andrew Hughes sat up.

"Sorry to wake you, Sir, but we have just received a message from our SOE agent at Spandau."

Andrew immediately asked what the message was. And the Corporal relayed Sharon's message. The implications were drastic.

"Get the Brigadier on the phone. And Thomas, can you get me a mug of sweet coffee?"

"Will do."

Andrew told the Brigadier that Sharon had overheard the Commandant at Spandau discussing plans with the top scientist to gather the files and be ready to leave at short notice. Apparently, the Commandant has reached out to both the Soviets and American intelligence for a guarantee of protection and resettlement, safe from any prosecution, in return for all their chemical weapons formulas. It would appear this Commandant wanted to do the deal with the Americans but was willing to trade with anyone to save his skin.

"Andrew, I need you to keep this to yourself for the time being. I will make some discrete enquiries, but you should know the flow of intelligence sharing between our allies and us has almost completely dried up."

"Aren't we supposed to be allies, trying to win this bloody war? "asked Andrew in total frustration.

"For some, it's now all about post-war positioning."

While things on the battlefront were starting to move fast. The allies' strategy now focused on taking Berlin and ending the war by April. This strategy meant allocating all available divisions to the Berlin objective. Bypassing southern Germany, effectively surrounding what few divisions Hitler had there. Once Berlin fell it was expected that the remaining German troops between southern Germany and Italy would immediately surrender. Given this change in direction, all SAS units were now being redeployed.

Ron saw a signpost indicating - 15 kilometres to Karlsruhe, and for the first time in the mission, he started to slightly relax. Rounding the sharp bend, they saw what everyone had been dreading. Ron immediately pumped his breaks in quick succession to alert Andy and Philip, and like the last time, they took steps to prepare for battle.

Nearing the roadblock, Ron slowed down. As he did, he switched on his headlights, not to blind the roadblock guards but to highlight their positions. The roadblock officer there ordered him to switch off the headlights. Ron complied, hoping that the others had enough time to identify their targets. The plan, should they be pulled over, was to slow to a stop and try and bluff their way through. If it was apparent that their cover was blown, Ian, with his already primed sub-machine gun, would spray the guards on the right side, and Philip from the sidecar would take the left. Ron and Andy would gun the engines. As soon as they passed the roadblock, Andy would overtake the staff car giving Philip and him as much protection with the car while Ian raked the area from the back window.

As they stopped, the guard's officer strode to the car with another guard close behind and another approaching the driver's side.

"Why are we being stopped?"

"My orders are to let no one pass."

"Your orders are to let no one retreat. We are heading towards the enemy, not running from him. Now clear the road, or you, and all your men, will find yourselves Gestapo prisoners."

"My orders are clear. I need you and all your passengers to get out of the car immediately."

His tone and his body language were clear. This officer was not going to back down. Ian saw the way the vehicles were parked to block the road. There was one weak point. He hoped Ron knew if the car in front was struck close to the boot, just to the right of the back wheel, it would pivot, clearing enough space for him to pass. And, at the same time, slam into the other car preventing it from pursuing them.

As Hans, the young German officer opened the front passenger side door to step out, he barked. "Get me your commanding officer on the phone, now."

For the first time, the guard's commanding officer looked worried. In that moment of hesitation, his men saw the panicked expression growing on his face. That split second was all it took for Ian to completely wipe out the two machine gun operators on his flank. He then cut down the other stunned guard before he had a chance to register the changed situation. Philip and Andy were firing on the position as Ron gunned the engine, thrusting the heavy car forward, easily brushing aside the rear of the nearest car blocking their path. Ian and Philip kept up a rain of bullets, buying enough time for Andy to follow through the gap Ron had cleared. Most of the guards had initially dived for cover and were only now returning inaccurate fire on the car.

They had just made it around the next bend, out of the line of fire, when Ron, from the car, noticed that Philip was completely doubled over and almost falling out of the sidecar.

"I think Philip's been hit," Ron said, then he noticed blood on the tunic of their young prisoner, Hans.

"Keep driving. We can't stop just yet."

A little further up ahead, Andy had pulled over and was helping Philip. Ron stopped, and Ian jumped out.

"We need to keep moving, Andy."

"He can't survive in the sidecar."

Ian knew Andy was right and helped him carry Philip to the back seat of the car. While Ron checked the young wounded officer.

"We need to get them immediate medical attention," Andy said.

"I know, but Karlsruhe is the nearest town."

"I think we will need to find something before that."

"I don't think there is anything," replied Ian.

They drove as fast as they could, constantly looking to see if there was a village, but as expected, there was nothing before the town. It was decided to park in a side street while Ian and Andy searched for a doctor's surgery. Once spotted, they knocked on the door several times before a sleepy old man opened the door. Andy quickly told him about the wounded men, and he, without hesitation, told them to bring them around to the ally leading to the rear of his surgery.

Within a minute of inspecting their wounds, he stabilised the young German officer. Then he focused his attention on the more seriously injured Philip.

Two hours passed slowly with Ian, and the doctor's wife assisting during both operations. Andy and Ron had decided to dump the vehicles, but before they did, they needed to hide the safe somewhere. On the drive to the doctors, they passed an old cemetery. Andy decided to backtrack and drop off the safe to be buried after they had hidden the vehicles. They then drove down the narrow lane beside the cemetery in the opposite direction from their planned escape route. Both men drove down the dirt road as far as they could then hid the vehicles in dense bushes, feeling confident they could not be seen from the main road. Returning to the graveyard, neither said anything, but both were acutely aware that the sky was getting lighter. Dawn would soon break, so they quickly selected an area near the corner wall next to a family plot. Both men committed the name Lehmann to memory agreeing not to write it down, just in case they were caught.

"Neither of your comrades can leave with you."

"They can't stay here. They will be caught and shot."

"If you move them, they will die."

"Is there anywhere we could hide them?"

"That one," pointing to the young officer, "I can move to my sister's house. He could get away with being her son recovering at home after being wounded. And this one can be taken to our asylum close to the river. I will arrange transport for both of them. But now you must leave, taking all their belongings and those blood-soaked bandages."

Ian gathered everything ready to go as soon as Andy and Ron returned. "I want to thank you and your wife. I will never forget your help."

"Go. I will keep your friends safe."

Ian scribbled a note to be hidden and given to the young German officer for him to use. If, or more likely, when he was taken prisoner by the advancing allied troops.

The three SAS troops left the others, both heavily medicated, and made a dash to the river. As they passed the graveyard, they saw the doctor helping the young German officer into his car. At the same time, the doctor's wife started scrubbing the stairs.

"What's she doing? It's a bit early for scrubbing the stairs," Andy said.

Ian smiled, "she's making sure no sniffer dog will go anywhere near the surgery. Not with that pungent chemical smell. They would rather run a mile than sniff those fumes."

As they passed the cemetery, Andy told Ian the family name beside where they had buried the safe.

Reaching the river, they could see the bridge and what appeared to be a total clampdown of traffic, and then they heard the dogs.

Chapter 43

Brigadier Gubbins phoned Colonel Hughes and arranged to meet him in Trafalgar Square. The crowds were milling around, and as usual, pigeons were flying amongst them, landing on outstretched arms, and pecking at the seeds in the proffered hands.

"What's up, Colin," Andrew asked.

"Things are moving fast, very fast."

"Yes, and from what I've heard, we could be in Berlin in the next week or two."

"We won't be."

"No?"

"This is top secret. Eisenhower has done a deal with Stalin to let the Soviets take Berlin."

"Churchill will be ropable."

"He doesn't know yet, and I can't tell him without exposing my contact. I know, amongst the few that are aware, overtures are being made to President Truman, but it appears he will back Eisenhour on this."

"What's the deal?"

"We don't know, and that's making me very nervous."

"If the Soviets take Berlin before we get there, they will capture Spandau Citadel, the scientists, and the chemical weapons formulas."

"That is why I need you to put a special covert team to get there first. But that team must be very discrete as this could easily blow up in our face."

"As you know, Colin, we have committed all our teams to special missions. These teams are widely spread out, operating from Norway, Greece, Yugoslavia, Italy, and France. I don't know if I can prepare a team in time."

"What about Captain Anderson. He knows Sharon. Can't you use him?"

"He's on a mission behind German lines. And the last I heard, he was, about to capture or kill Karl Barbie in a Chateau just outside of Stuttgart. His orders were once they had completed the mission, they were to head back to their rendezvous with our SAS team there."

"You need to get in touch with him, and I need you to get up to our front command post in Leipzig, ready to brief a snatch team. Our Commanders are about to be told their objective has changed, and they will not be advancing on Berlin. You don't have much time left, but you will need to set up a jump-off point for the mission to Spandau. The situation is very fluid, but I will keep you informed. And Andrew, I can't stress enough that you can't mention the mission to anyone."

"I understand. I will make contact with them immediately, and get back to you as soon as I have."

Ian knew it would be too dangerous to try and cross the river in broad daylight. He also knew this sector of the river offered the safest crossing.

"Ron, I want you to stay here with the backpacks. If we are not back by dark, hide what you can't take in that tree trunk and float over with what you can. Some files are better than no files, and you can also direct people to where the safe is."

Ron nodded, and Ian, along with Andy, made their way back to the outskirts of the town. They found a secure vantage point and waited. As expected, a convoy of vehicles filled with troops started arriving. The officers were clearly unhappy to be so close to the advancing allied armies. But the senior officer ordered half of them to begin searching the village and make a house-to-house search. Addressing the remaining troops, he split them into two groups, with one group to head north of the bridge and the others south.

"What are they waiting for? Why haven't they started their search?" asked Andy.

Before Ian could answer, they saw what he had dreaded. Three dogs.

"Let's get back to Ron and work out our next move."

Planning the next move was taken out of their hands. They heard the barking and snarling. The handlers were holding the dogs on a tight lead when one of the handlers tripped and let go of the dog's lead. The dog raced towards Ian and Andy. Both knew they could not outrun the dog, so they took up a firing position and waited for it to crash through the scrub at any moment, when they heard a pathetic squeal. The dog's lead had caught around a fallen tree branch, and the sudden stop wrenched back its neck as it leapt over the fallen tree. They could still hear the dog's painful cry's until a single shot silenced the poor animal. One thing was sure no other dog would be let off the lead unless there was a clear line of sight.

Both men were up and sprinting back to where Ron had taken up a covering firing position. Looking through his sniper scope, he saw there were another two, now terrified, anxious dogs.

"I can make the shot on one of the other dog handlers," Ron said.

"Take it," was Ian's immediate reply.

The shot rang out, and the dog handler experienced a moment of confusion and then died before his brain had registered what had just happened to him.

In that instance, the others in the group threw themselves to the ground. The two dogs, now totally confused, pulled at their leads, trying to move handlers, one lying scared to move and the other lying dead.

Ian stood up and started firing, not so much trying to hit anything, simply wanting to add confusion and chaos amongst their pursuers.

Further up at the bridge, armed patrol boats were being launched. Ian grabbed one of the packs and started moving towards the enemy forces.

"Should we not try heading south?" Ron asked.

"That's what they will expect us to do. We are heading back into town."

Chapter 44

Hiding again on the outskirts of the town, Ian told Andy and Ron that they should head east and then circle back south towards the river. If at all possible, they should not engage enemy patrols.

"We need them to think we are all still together heading north."

"Why don't we stick together?" Ron asked.

"If we split, we double our chance of getting these files back and later retrieving the buried safe."

"What's your plan?" Andy asked.

Ian made it clear he was initially going to attack them using the sniper rifle. Then I will use my Submachine gun and pistol to try and convince them they were facing more than one shooter. Ian also gathered whatever explosives, detonators and tripwires they still had. After handing over all their explosives, both Andy and Ron gave Ian their spare pistol ammunition.

"You need to keep two pistol magazines for yourselves. Hopefully, you don't have to use them."

Placing the spare ammo and explosives in his small backpack Ian wished them the best of luck then the group split, moving in different directions.

Ian took to the high ground but never broke the ridge. He found an ideal spot where he could see the lead German patrol. The one with the two dogs. From where he was, Ian had the best sniper position but knew he would have to move as soon as he fired. He had already picked out the next best spot but surmised a half-decent officer would also see that as a likely position and have his troops ready to fire on it. That left the low bushes just at the edge of the woods. He would have to get there before they could clear their vulnerable position, and that would mean sliding twenty feet down the steep gravel slope. Ian would have to be able to grab and hold on to that clump of bushes, or he might find himself sliding over the edge to an unknown drop.

Sorry about this, Ian thought to himself as he aimed then slowly squeezed the sniper rifle's trigger. Not waiting to see if he had hit the dog, Ian threw himself onto the slope. The incline was steeper than he thought, and he only just managed to snag the bush with the butt of his rifle.

Quickly scrambling to a firing position, he saw the dog and dog handler racing for the vehicle. The shot was at a much more acute angle, and Ian had to fire three shots before he hit the dog. And then the ground all around him started spitting dirt. As heavy machine gun rounds were smashing into the ground all about him, Ian knew the troops would be rushing up the slope towards him.

From where he was, he could not see over the edge. *If this is a sheer drop, I'm in deep shit, he thought as he let go of the bush and started to slide.*

Andy and Ron were travelling fast when they encountered the first patrol on their journey south. Both men felt confident they could take out this patrol but knew that would give their plan away, so they lay still with their silenced pistols at the ready.

The German patrol's radio crackled then they heard the operator speaking. As soon as the message was finished, the officer standing next to the operator demanded a report.

"The front search party have come under sniper fire and are calling for all patrols to swiftly close the net on the saboteurs. Patrols are moving west from the town, and we are to keep boats in the water and quickly push up the riverbank. They are confident we have them cornered."

The officer sent a runner to the boat crews, blew his whistle, and signalled to the others on foot to start moving forward in an extended line. Andy and Ron had just enough time to find a hiding place next to some fallen moss-covered trees. Luckily for them, troops would find it difficult to keep an extended line, with some having an easy path while others having to cut through overgrowth and climb over fallen trees.

And, as many training exercises had demonstrated, those with the more arduous path were much less attentive in the search. They had to fight hard just to keep up with the line.

Ian slipped over the edge, fearing the worst, But as luck would have it, he landed on a three-foot-wide ledge. With no time to spare, he was on the move. Ian had no time to look back as the bang from the mortar shell exploded where he had been less than a minute ago.

He deliberately moved much closer to the hunters. Now the cat and mouse game was on. And Ian knew he would be glad of all those torturous hours of evasion training in the Scottish Highlands.

The theory was simple, set up your trip wires and draw them towards you. The execution was where things got more complicated when they could come at you from various angles. Still, Ian hoped that after the first explosive went off, killing those around it, ihe other hunters would become far more cautious and thus slow down.

Ian did not have to wait long for the section patrolling to his left to be nearly upon him. Timing was going to be everything. You have to let some pass before firing on them, hopefully drawing them towards you.

His plan worked like a textbook exercise. Initially, the patrol took cover, then sensing rather than seeing Ian's retreat, they fanned out and started advancing in his direction. The explosion, when it happened, threw the patrol into total confusion. Injured troops were screaming or crying out for help, while those uninjured were scared to move, worried that more tripwires were set. A worry that was justified, when, after the patrol leader regained control, and, sent a recovery squad. As they carefully approached their wounded comrades, one gently moved aside a fallen branch noticing too late the thin trip wire.

The German officer in command knew instinctively that his inexperienced troops were out of their depth and had now become the hunted rather than the hunters.

Ian felt he had inflicted enough carnage on his pursuers and decided now was the time to look for a safe hiding place until darkness fell.

Meanwhile Andy and Ron had reached the river and were surprised to see two of the boats heading north, leaving only one with two troopers on board and four on shore.

"What do you reckon, Andy, can should we risk it?"

"No, we have to wait until it's dark. It would only take one of the patrol to turn around and catch a glimpse of us trying to cross, and we would literally be dead in the water."

"Do you think the SAS unit will still be waiting for us?" Ron asked.

"I bloody hope so. That's what we agreed on."

Corporal Williams rushed into Colonel Hughes's office. "Sir, the SAS patrol needs to speak to you."

"Yes!" Hughes snapped into the receiver.

"Sir, we have been ordered to vacate the area and make our way back to Nancy, a town about 100 miles west of Strasbourg, for redeployment to the Elbe River just south of Hamburg."

"When?"

"Now. We have been ordered to leave immediately."

"And what about my people? They will be expecting you at the rendezvous?"

"I have raised this with our commander, but he insists on us leaving immediately. I don't have his approval, but I can leave them a vehicle, some supplies, and a radio. I am sorry, Colonel, that's the best I can do."

"Leave them as much as you can," Hughes hung up and immediately contacted the Brigadier's office.

"What's happening, Colin? I've got Ian Anderson and his team heading for a rendezvous with no one there to meet them. The SAS unit has been pulled out."

"The German lines in the west are collapsing, and the orders are to leave the south until after Berlin falls."

"Have plans changed? Are we going to take Berlin?"

"No, we won't. It's still being left for the Soviets to take. Our orders are to take Hamburg and Rostock and not to cross the Elbe River. Have you managed to make contact with Anderson's team yet?"

"No. I have heard from the MI6 field agent. She said Ian's team left in the early hours of the morning and believed they would be crossing the Rhine tonight if they managed to evade German patrols."

"Do you think they will have evaded the patrols?"

"If anyone can, it's them."

"Okay, I will order that SAS team back to the rendezvous and hope Ian is there to meet them. And, if the Germans have completely vacated the area, I will get a plane to Nancy to pick up Ian and fly him to meet you at Leipzig. Time is running out."

As Andrew Hughes was absorbing the latest details. Sharon made contact. Her coded message was clear. The Soviets are making inroads into Berlin. If we are to make an extraction, it must be very soon.

Hughes quickly drafted a reply telling her to get as many explosives onto the site as possible and hide them, ready should we need them. He also needed her to find out where the formulas were being kept. Andrew told Sharon to destroy the files if all else failed.

Sharon told the Colonel she had also drawn up a map of where best to place the explosives, should she need to cripple the plant. He also told her to stand by every night.

Ian started moving as soon as the sky darkened. He had formulated his plan, which required him to stage a massive diversionary attack. Hoping the German patrol would further concentrate their efforts here, leaving the escape route for Andy and Ron unguarded. Reluctantly Ian discarded the sniper rifle, hiding it under thick scrub. He carried out a final check of his small backpack. There were sufficient explosives and detonators for what he needed. Once ready to move, he picked up the remainder of his gear, his sub-machine gun with two magazines, his pistol and knife.

The patrols had pulled back to their makeshift camp, for the night, Ian quickly checked their sentries' posts. The troops there were tired and inattentive. Ian easily slipped past them and found the camp generator and fuel supply, wasting no time rigging up concealed explosives set to go off in thirty minutes. Next, he looked for their ammunition dump and almost bumped into its sole guard. Time was not on Ian's side. He had to set the explosives and get clear before they went off. He knew he would have to silence the sentry. Discarding all his gear except his Fairbairn and Sykes knife, he slowly deliberately crept towards the lone sentry.

He couldn't remember how many times he had practised this very technique at night in darkness, during training in Scotland? Although he had practised the technique, and had killed many in battle, he knew he would never get used to the revulsion he felt when actually sticking his knife into an unsuspecting guard. The thought of grabbing someone and pushing your knife to the hilt into their exposed neck almost made him want to pull back. *Don't be a hypocrite. Just think of all the agents and commandos you have taught to perform this very act. Now do it.* The guard looked very young, and Ian had to suppress his feeling of revulsion. He cupped his hand over the guard's mouth and quickly, wanting to get it over with, pushed the knife into the exposed neck. The guard gurgled and then slumped in his arms. Ian hoped this boy, for he was just a boy, was dead even before his brain registered what had happened. Very carefully, Ian laid the guard on the ground behind a pile of empty ammunition boxes and covered him with one of the tarpaulins lying around.

Ian wondered how, or if, he would be able to reconcile his actions once the war was over. But that would have to wait. He had to do whatever it took to give Andy and Ron the best chance to escape. Then without any more self-reprisals, he set the explosives timed to synchronise with the fuel dump charges. Knowing he could not help Andy and Ron anymore, it was his time to get out of there.

What surprised Ian was the level of vehicle activity. At first, he thought it would be more difficult getting across the bridge with the number of troops on guard duty. But after studying the guard's movements, he saw their blind spot. His escape would require him to reach the bridge anchor point halfway up the bank, climb through the brace structure to reach just below the road, and scramble across the bridge without being spotted.

Ian managed to reach the bridge and started to climb. He nearly fell when he stood on something soft, which moved, causing him to slip. Protecting himself from falling, his machine gun struck against the iron struts. The bump caused a high-pitched metallic ping.

Two guards, close by, immediately looked up. They made their way to just below Ian as one of the guards shone his torch. Ian froze and then saw the rat he had stood on now inches from his hand. If he let go, he would lose his balance, but the outcome would be the same if the rat bit him. Below the guard was still shining his torch from section to section, and it was only a matter of seconds before he would be illuminated. The rat's attention was dragged from Ian to the torch beam, and in that fraction of a second, Ian sharply brushed the rat off the beam. It squealed as it fell, narrowly missing the guard, who, in panic, dropped his torch and jumped back. Seeing the rat scurrying into the river, the guard picked up his now broken torch. Still recovering from the fright they had just had, both guards hurriedly walked away from the riverbank without a further glance back.

Having reached a position high enough in the structure where Ian felt comfortable to move off from the anchored side and start to cross the span of the river when he spotted the explosive charge. *Christ, they've rigged the bridge for demolition.*

Earlier that day German engineers had prepared the bridge for destruction should the allies advance towards Stuttgart and Munich. Ian, starting to panic knowing if they set the explosives off while he was on the bridge he would be blown to smithereens. He checked his watch, not sure how much time he might have. Hoping the German engineers would leave the bridge intact as an escape route for their retreating forces. He did not want to slow his getaway down but knew he couldn't ignore the explosive. Not only because if they blew the bridge it would hinder the allies' advance, but not wanting to think about it, blow him to bits. Ian examined the cluster of charges, cut the wires, and removed the detonators, dropping them into the river. As he moved between them, crossing the width of the bridge to the other side, he again removed the detonators. Had these charges exploded, the bridge would have been unpassable. The question going through his head was whether there were other clusters. Halfway over, he got the answer to that niggling question. As before, he cut the wires and removed the detonators. That was when the fuel dump exploded, followed by the ammunition dump. Ian could only imagine the panic now playing out in the camp.

As darkness crept in, Andy and Ron slipped into the river. With their packs tied onto a large clump of bush acting as a float and giving them cover, they started gently swimming to the other bank. They were almost halfway there when they heard a massive explosion followed a minute later by another. Ron smiled at Andy.

"I guess Ian's up and about."

The SAS unit were about to leave the rendezvous area when they were given new orders to wait for the others. Their orders emphasised the importance of getting Ian's team to Nancy, where a plane would be waiting for them. Given the last-minute change in orders, the SAS unit settled into position to wait for Ian's team.

Andy and Ron arrived at the rendezvous and were immediately informed of the new orders.

"Ian planned to use the bridge to cross the river at Karlsruhe, then fallow the riverbank pathway to here. So I'm going to make my way along the pathway to the bridge to meet up with him. I need you guys to stay here and be ready to leave as soon as we return," Ian said.

"I'll come along with you," said Ron.

"No, it's best that you stay here with the files, in case things go south. You need to be able to inform the Brigadier about the safe and its location."

"Okay, but we will be here when you both return."

It had been slow, hard going and with aching legs, Ian wondered if he would get to the other side before daylight. Finally reaching the other end, he was glad to see no guards were patrolling the area. Stiffly he made his way down to the riverbank and, to his surprise, saw Andy waiting.

"You took your time," Andy said with a broad smile stretched across his face.

"I stopped halfway for some breakfast," Ian replied.

During his crossing, Ian noticed the traffic noise had eased up, and was not surprised when he found out the Germans had retreated and were setting up their defences on that side of the Rhine.

"The SAS boys can give us a lift to Nancy," Andy said.

"What's in Nancy?"

"A plane to fly us to Leipzig."

"Leipzig, why?"

"That's where Colonel Hughes will be."

"I'm confused. I thought he would want us back in London right away."

"They do. Well, they want Ron in London immediately, but you and I are to head to Leipzig."

"I need to speak to the Colonel," Ian said.

"You can't. He's on a flight himself."

Chapter 45

After meeting up with the SAS unit, they made their way cautiously back to Strasbourg. From there, it was about 70 miles as the crow fly's, to Nancy, a lot further by windy forest roads. It was unclear if the Germans had completely evacuated the area. So, no one could relax. About halfway to Nancy, the front vehicle skidded to a halt. Everyone was on high alert as the driver went to check the fallen tree for booby traps. As he bent to look down, the driver in the second jeep was shot in the forehead and died instantly. Both vehicles were empty in seconds, and all eyes searched for the enemy sniper. The driver of the first jeep crawled towards the ditch at the side of the dirt track, trying to reach cover when he was hit in the shoulder. Ian saw where he thought the sniper was, and, opened up with his machine gun, giving the wounded driver enough cover fire for him to finally reach the ditch. A shot from another angle slammed into the side of the jeep, trying to immobilise it. Those on the right side of the dirt road were pinned down, but fortunately, the others had cover and could move. Ian believed there were at least two snipers, and he had a good idea where one was perched.

He crawled to his right while Andy and two of the SAS squad moved left. Both Ian and Andy had rehearsed

this type of ambush evasion numerous times, so there was no need for verbal communication.

The snipers had the advantage of a superior weapon. But they had made a classic mistake of choosing the best but most obvious firing position. And due to the snipers' relative closeness, Ian knew they could reign devastating fire on their position and would soon immobilise the jeeps. Ian knew he had to get closer to return effective fire. Again, one of the snipers broke cover to fire into the side of the jeep, trying to explode the petrol tank. His movement gave Andy a fleeting chance of a shot. He did not miss. The other sniper fired on Andy's position, but he had already rolled to his left and taken cover behind a dead tree trunk.

Ian had managed to crawl even closer to the second sniper's position. He was confident the sniper could not see him. Andy appeared to move from his cover, as the bushes parted, the sniper fired. Feeling under pressure, the sniper started to draw back from his position. As he turned to move, Ian stood up and fired four shots into his chest. The sniper's face registered shocked surprise. And slowly fell backwards, toppling over the edge of the hilly overhang, and landing close to the bush where Andy had recently tricked him into firing at.

Ian collected both dead snipers' rifles and ammunition in case they needed them.

Back at the jeeps, the SAS unit had taken care of their wounded comrade and had placed and covered their fallen comrade on the back of the second jeep.

After checking both vehicles, they cleared the road and once more headed to Nancy.

When they arrived at Nancy, they were surprised to see the number of troops gathered there, protecting the two-light aircraft. The first was scheduled to take Ron back to London, and the SAS unit leader asked that pilot if he would take back his dead comrade.

"Of course."

"Captain Anderson?" asked the other pilot.

"Yes."

"I've got the pleasure of flying you to Leipzig."

"The pleasure, I think, is mine."

"But before we depart, you have to call this number," the pilot handed Ian a piece of paper. "There's a phone in that shop," pointing to a general store.'

Ian called the number and was surprised to hear Corporal Williams answering his call.

"Is the Colonel there?"

"Yes."

Andrew took the offered phone. "Ian, great to hear from you."

"Andrew."

"I can't go into details on the phone, but as soon as I get the chance, I will bring you up to speed with breaking developments."

"Can we talk on the radio while I'm in flight?"

"No, unfortunately, that's even less secure."

"Okay."

"Ian, it is imperative that neither you nor Andy demonstrates any recognition of me when we meet in Leipzig."

"This sounds very ominous."

"Believe me, it's a game changer."

Epilogue

The phone rang and Brigadier Gubbins answered immediately.

"Where are we at, Andrew?"

"We have been strong-armed into including OSS officers on the Spandau mission. I tried to tell them this was a British only operation but..."

"I know. I saw the report. Did you manage to speak to Ian?"

"Briefly, just before he left. But I have managed to speak in more detail to Sharon. She gave a reasonable description of the Citadel's layout, and I have passed that on to Ian for his and Sergeant Fyfe's eyes only."

"Andrew, all the intelligence reports predict Berlin, and therefore Spandau Citadel and their chemical weapons research plant, will be in the Soviets' hands within the week."

"Then let us pray Ian and his team succeed."

Don't miss out!

Visit the website below and you can sign up to receive emails whenever Les McLaughlan publishes a new book. There's no charge and no obligation.

https://books2read.com/r/B-A-VKPT-TGKMC

BOOKS 2 READ

Connecting independent readers to independent writers.

Also by Les McLaughlan

Project Damocles
Spandau Citadel
Craigmarr's Lament
Churchill's Secret Saboteurs

About the Author

Born in Glasgow, Les has lived more of his life in Perth, Western Australia, than in Scotland, yet his accent is still so strong some people think he has just stepped off the boat. He moved to Perth in 1978.

A licensed electrician who worked on many large construction projects. Les went to work for the Electrical Trade Union in 1990 and went on to become the State Secretary in 2006 until 2017.

He is married with two children, two grandchildren, and his best friend Rebus a Border Collie.